LEAH BEACH

To Those Who Wander

To my mother who wholeheartedly believes in in the idea of love and my father who subscribes to the theory of soulmates. Thank you for showing me all the ways that love can persevere and perish. The ways that it can mold and cherish. Without you two, I wouldn't know love—much less be able to write about it.

Contents

Acknowledgement

As always, thank you to my wonderful husband. Nick, you don't know everything you do that helps to keep me writing. Without you, I would have quit before I even started.

Of course I couldn't have finished this novel without my tried and true proofreaders, Angela and Kirstan. You two are the best ever.

Thank you to my parents for the unconditional love that has gotten me through the hard times and shone out of me during the good ones.

I can't even begin to convey my gratitude for the rest of my family—aunts, uncle, grandmother—you all know who you are. From throwing me a book signing party for my debut novel to just checking in on me through a quick text, you're always there and I love you all.

Chapter 1

Grace

I've never felt anything this hot. My fingers feel like they're burning with every brush against his skin.

"You really need to start wearing more sunscreen. This sunburn is horrible," I say as I continue to rub the aloe into the lobster currently under my hands.

"We can't all have your gorgeous permanent tan," Weston replies, sighing loudly.

I guess I did get lucky in that department. Having a Spanish father with dominant genes gives me a beautiful year-round skin color. But, I still wear sunscreen. Wes doesn't seem inclined to listen to my reasoning right now, however.

The grumbles emanating from the man on the couch are making it hard to keep a straight face. "Listen, you gotta stop or I'm not going to be able to continue. And I happen to know you can't reach this spot between your shoulder blades, judging by how much more burnt it is than the rest of your back. You know you could've asked, I would have helped you out."

"I felt weird asking. Just because we're friends and basically together all the time doesn't mean you want to also have to put sunscreen on me," Weston replies, face still smushed into the pillow.

I feel a blush steal across my face, immediately grateful that Wes can't see me right now. I hate when he reminds me of our friendship. Not that I don't love being his friend, I just sometimes wish we could be more. But I know he only sees me as Brian's ex-girlfriend. Even though they're not in contact as often now, Wes is still so loyal that I know he wouldn't make a move on his "friend's girl." Never mind the fact that I'm the one that ended the relationship.

I shake my head, pushing my thoughts back to the current moment. Catching myself just before I started to dip my fingers into the back of Weston's shorts. My hands still on his back, shocked by the betrayal of my body. I sit back sharply and in what I can only imagine is a squeak of a sound, I say, "Okay, all done. I'm heading back to my place now."

Weston pushes his upper body off of the couch, exploiting every muscle and drawing my traitorous eyes to each one. I quickly step away, darting my gaze away as he sits up to face me.

"I thought you wanted to grab a drink? Aren't Amanda and Patrick watching a movie at your place?" Wes asks, still not reaching to put on the shirt that's sitting right beside him. He can't possibly know how I'm feeling right now, but I really need him to cover himself. Even reddened from the sun, his chest is a masterpiece of musculature.

With my eyes downcast, I relent. "Yeah, sure we could still go for a drink. Can I use your bathroom to freshen up real quick?"

I catch movement out of my peripheral vision and I look up in time to see Weston standing right in front of me, stooped down to try to catch my eyes.

"Are you okay? You seem...put out all of a sudden. If you don't want to have a drink with me, I totally understand."

I scrub my hand over my face and try to tell myself to get over this stupidity I'm feeling. "No Wes, I'd love to go for a drink. Really. Just let me run in here and I'll be back." I smile, unable to make it reach my eyes. He still seems troubled by my change in attitude as I walk away.

Get a grip on yourself, I silently lecture. Just because he doesn't want to be with me doesn't mean I need to ruin this friendship.

Chapter 2

Weston

I'm left a little confused as Grace walks away to the bathroom. We were just talking and joking like normal and then she got all weird. This has been happening some recently, on both sides of the conversation. But I don't know how to change it.

I'm attracted to her and I don't know how to tell her. Spending the last year together, traveling from hospital to hospital on contracts has been so fun and I don't want that to end because I do something stupid.

I don't know that she's over Brian. We don't talk about that kind of stuff a lot. Maybe I could ask her tonight though. The worst part is, I know why she broke up with him. If she's not wanting to be in a relationship, how can I ruin our friendship by asking her to be in one?

I'm pulled out of my thoughts by Grace's return. She looks so beautiful today. Well, she looks beautiful everyday. But today for the group hike and boat cruise she wore a white skirt and cream tank over her bikini. You can see glimpses of her tan skin through the macrame of the top and her luscious black hair is swept over her shoulder and hanging in loose curls down her back. I honestly don't know how someone can be out in the sun all day and still look that gorgeous.

She catches me staring for a moment too long and asks, "Are you coming or are your brain cells fried along with your skin?"

I bark out a laugh, making her smile and reply, "Sorry, I was lost in thought. Let's go kill some more of those brain cells."

The best thing about this island? Strong-ass drinks.

Once we're seated at the bar of the closest restaurant, we order some Painkillers to get our night started.

"So Lexa and Drew, huh?" I say, startling Grace out of her train of thought.

"Oh, I know right? It's not like we didn't already know. But seeing them together—they are just perfect."

"Yeah, they've been putting that off for way too long," I say, thinking back on the years of conversations I've had with both of our friends concerning their feelings for each other.

"It's all about timing," Grace says, frowning into her near-empty drink.

Timing? Maybe that's the thing holding us back for now. I can wait. Hell, Drew waited nearly a decade for Lexa. I can wait until Grace is ready for a relationship again.

I open my mouth, intending to ask Grace how she's feeling about her relationship status but I never get the chance.

"I think I'm ready to start dating again," she blurts, still not turning to look at me.

I stare at the side of her face until she finally shifts enough to allow eye contact. "Yeah?" I say, unable to formulate any other response.

"Yeah," she sighs with relief. "I think it's time and I'm

ready. I was the one who ended things with Brian. I knew it was coming."

"True, but you two had been together for a long time. I hope you don't feel like you have to rush into anything."

"I mean, I'm obviously not ready to settle down. I just want to have some fun for a while. See what or who all is out there," she says, staring over my shoulder.

Oh. She's not talking about me.

"Ready for another?" the bartender asks, gesturing towards my empty glass.

"Oh, sure," I say, absently. I hadn't even realized I finished it already. I reach for my new drink, still thinking about Grace's comment. I want her but I don't know if I can do a fling. *Good thing she never asked you for one,* I remind myself.

Chapter 3

Grace

It's hard to tell what's running through Weston's mind right now, but it has him very quiet. I didn't realize that telling him I was thinking about dating again would shut down our ability to have a conversation.

We've been hanging out—just the two of us—for almost a year now. After Ansley's wedding last year, we ended up taking travel nursing contracts near each other. We met up several times to have dinner, see movies and all the other things friends do together. After that contract was over, we decided to find one at the same hospital and started looking for two bedroom apartments with short term rental options.

Over the past year we've been to 4 different states together and now we're in St. Croix on vacation. But still not *together*. Of course, I've been thinking that if he was interested, he would have made a move by now. But maybe he's trying to leave that up to me.

Which is why I said I was ready to date. Or have something fun. I'm not sure what he'd rather do but I don't want to pressure him into anything. But it's like my announcement upset him somehow. Maybe he's really not that into me.

"Watcha thinkin' about?" I ask, trying to draw Wes back into a conversation.

"Oh, um, just plans for when we get back. Our contract ends in 4 weeks. Have you thought about your next destination?" he asks.

I shake my head, but don't respond aloud. I didn't realize there wouldn't be another "where are we going next" discussion. It sounds more like he's completely shutting down the idea of us still traveling together.

"I saw some places near Chicago that were looking for OR and ICU nurses. Then we'd be close to Claire and Jackson for a little while," I say, trailing off a bit at the blank look on Wes's face.

"I don't know that I'm wanting to continue to travel. I've been thinking about settling somewhere," Weston says. He won't meet my eye anymore and it's making me nervous.

"Oh, okay. Well, then I have no idea. Maybe I'll still go to Chicago. We haven't been to an Illinois hospital yet. May I ask, when did you decide you didn't want to travel any longer?" I ask, still confused by the strange tension between us.

"I don't know. It was just a thought. I don't mind continuing to travel, especially if I have a built-in buddy at the hospital," he replies, finally making eye contact and giving me a goofy smile.

"Mkay, right. Like you don't make friends easily enough," I sarcastically respond.

Chapter 4

Weston

Why am I continuing to make this awkward? It's not like she told me she's married and moving in with someone else. She only said that she was ready for casual relationships again. That's not that big of a deal. Right?

But I don't know that I can share an apartment with her while she's bringing people home.

I shift my hips on the bar stool to open my upper body towards Grace. I let out a breath and a prayer and say, "Grace, I would love to continue traveling with you. Are you still wanting to share a space?"

Grace's cheeks are rosy, though I don't know if it's from the drinks, the heat or the conversation. "Of course I still want to share an apartment. It's fun having you for a roommate and rent is a lot cheaper," she says, winking and smiling.

"Oh, so the rent is your only concern then?" I ask, laughing.

"Well obviously I love having a big, strong man around. To open the pickle jars and unstick the doors when it's humid."

"I have a feeling you could manage those things on your own.

I've watched you change your own tires and I don't know that you've ever met a jar you couldn't open," I reply, giving Grace my best smirk.

"You're right. I guess I just enjoy your company. Sue me," she says, laughing.

I shake my head, smile in place. On the inside though, I wish she wanted more than just my presence.

As soon as our second drinks are downed—in record time—we gingerly slide off of our bar stools. Those Painkillers really pack a punch.

I look at Grace, brown eyes slightly glazed and cheeks painted a beautiful pink and can't stop the thoughts from bubbling up. Or out of my mouth. "God, you're gorgeous," I say, before slamming my lips shut.

Grace's face turns bright red before she rips her gaze from mine. Still looking at her feet, she mumbles, "Thanks, Wes."

"Sorry, I didn't mean to be weird. I just thought you should know," I say, trying to save some face.

Grace thankfully brings her eyes back to mine and her face lights up with a smile. "I say silly things when I'm drunk, too. I just didn't know you were such a lightweight."

I laugh but don't try to argue. I'd rather she think I'm just tipsy than know that she's all I really think about anymore.

Chapter 5

Grace

We walk back towards our separate villas in relative silence. The sound of waves crashing onto the shore breaking into my thoughts. I don't realize that Weston is trying to walk me back to my place until we're standing at the door.

"Well, here we are," he says, gesturing to the door. I can hear the sounds of a fast-paced action movie blaring through the wood, so Amanda and Patrick are still doing movie night.

"Any chance of a nightcap at your place? They're still watching that new action movie in there and I won't be able to think with how loud I know Amanda watches things." *She really should just use closed captions*, I think to myself.

"Sure! Follow me," Weston says, waving his hand over his shoulder.

"Yeah, um, I've been there. But sure, I'll follow you," I say, snarky as ever.

Weston just rolls his eyes and strikes up a conversation over the last movies we've seen. "Remember the one with the pig? And the little boots? I think that one is my new favorite," he says, unironically.

Of course I remember it, he laughed and smiled the entire movie. I found it extremely cute and endearing. "Yes, Weston. I remember. It was alright."

As he types in his key code and swings the door open, he places his hand on my lower back. Tingles immediately shoot up my spine and I go semi-rigid. I can tell that he feels the tremor because he shoots a look at me out of the corner of his eye.

"Sorry?" he says, question in his voice.

"No, you're good. Just got a chill all of a sudden." I don't want him to think he can't touch me. Only because I want him to touch me. *Get it together woman,* I chide myself. It's just the alcohol talking...I hope.

"What are you in the mood for? Wine, beer, whiskey? I have some of the local rum in here, too." I watch as Wes rummages through the alcohol options in the cabinet. This place really does stock everything.

"Definitely not rum," I respond, laughing. "Those drinks at the bar were a little too strong. Maybe just a beer?"

"Gotcha. I think I'll have one of those as well." My mouth gapes open a bit as I watch the muscles ripple underneath the soft t-shirt Wes is wearing. I didn't realize it took so many muscle groups to open a beer bottle. Not that I am in any way complaining about the sight.

I can't control the way my mouth drops open or the way my eyes are devouring the man in front of me. Not even when Wes turns, catching me in the act.

"Grace? You, uh, okay over there?" Wes asks, seeming to trip over his words.

When I finally rip my gaze from his body and meet his eyes,

I'm stunned by the heat behind them. His normally light brown eyes are buried beneath his widened pupils, his mouth parted with his heavy breathing.

"Wes," I breath, not having the opportunity to say more before he's made it across the room and thrust his hand into my hair. We are sharing the same breath, eyes clashing in widened stares, both searching for a no but praying for a yes.

Just as Weston leans his face down to mine, his lips mere inches from my own, the door bursts open.

"What's up party people?!" Patrick shouts, effectively ruining my life.

Wes and I step back from each other, but can't seem to break eye contact as Pat continues to ramble about the movie he just watched.

Weston turns to face his friend, subtle anger etched into his features. Patrick is too busy to notice, still caught up in his retelling. Abashed, I make my exit towards the front door, grabbing my beer from the kitchen on the way out.

I turn once, as I'm closing the door, and I meet Weston's eyes again. They're full of regret and that kills me. I wish he didn't regret almost kissing me.

Chapter 6

Weston

"You have got to have the worst timing in the world," I say to Patrick, still not looking away from the door Grace just ran through.

Patrick pauses his narrative long enough to look at my face, seeing frustration there. "Oh sorry dude, did I interrupt something?" He looks genuinely sorry, but that doesn't help my mood. I almost got to kiss Grace. She almost let me. What does this mean? We had a few drinks tonight, but she didn't by any means seem drunk. But the way she was looking at me when I turned around, there was no denying the unchecked desire I saw.

It's taking everything in me not to rush out the door after her. But the look on her face when she left–after the desire cooled–was fear. I can't run her down and force her to kiss me when she's afraid to even want me. I need so badly to talk to her about this, but maybe tomorrow. We have a full day of sightseeing and shopping.

Speaking of, I should probably try to get some sleep. This

sunburn is starting to feel painful again and I need some rest.

I know I won't be able to sleep very easily though, not with the ghost of Grace's hands and scent on me.

➻

I can't believe I slept at all last night with the vivid dreams I was having. Living in the same apartment as Grace while we travel has given me insight into her behavior that I know most don't see. I have seen what she looks like when she's just woken up, when she's gotten all dolled up to go out with friends, when she's on the couch in her favorite sweatpants. It's hard to say which version has intrigued me the most, but my subconscious played them on a loop for me last night. This is part of the reason I suggested we look at separate contracts for the next assignment, I've been having these dreams for months. But none of my dream versions of Grace match up to what I saw when I was awake last night. I still can't get her heated brown eyes, her slightly parted lips and her small, quick breaths out of my head.

I need to get a handle on myself if I'm going to be spending all day around her and the rest of our friends. Today is our last full day in St. Croix, and thankfully we're spending it inside shops and riding in air conditioned vehicles. I am still way too burnt to handle more sun.

It takes longer than I would have liked to roll my ass out of bed and start getting dressed. Between the burn and the energy I expended in my sleep, I am going to need a heaping cup of coffee to get this day going.

With a groan, I make my way to my feet, scrubbing my hands down my face. I swipe some Tylenol from the nightstand on my way to the bathroom, attempting to ward off the headache I can already feel forming between my brows.

A nice cold shower is calling my name and I'm happy to answer. Throwing back some water, I swallow the Tylenol and turn on the shower. I step into the spray, eyes closed and body tensed for the cold. The water feels amazing on my skin though, so I quickly release the tension from my muscles and let the shower do its job. It's currently serving the dual purpose of cooling off my heated skin and putting a simmer on my frazzled nerves.

I don't feel like taking my time this morning when all I really care to do is hang out with Grace some more.

I quickly run through my routine—shampoo, condition and gingerly scrub my skin clean. I feel like the lotion Grace applied last night helped soothe some of the burn.

I shut off the shower stream, stepping out into the bathroom. I am too used to my stinging hot showers that fog up the mirrors, because my crystal clear reflection startles me. I catch my own gaze and note that the burn has actually eased some from yesterday, starting to turn into a bit of a tan already. A pink tan, but at least I no longer resemble Larry the Lobster.

We're meeting in our common area in about 10 minutes, so I really only have time to throw on some clothes and grab a quick breakfast. With that thought comes a deep rumble from my stomach. I laugh, realizing I'll need to grab some food while we're out, probably. I slip into some loose athletic shorts and a tank top and head to the kitchen. I put some coffee on and walk to the fridge to see what I have available. Looking over my choices, I select an apple and grab a banana from the counter. I toss some ice and creamer into a cup and wait at the coffee maker for my brew to finish.

I'm halfway through my apple when Patrick waltzes into the kitchen, looking like he just walked off of an island chic runway.

"They make those clothes for us common folk too, your majesty?" I ask, quirking an eyebrow at my temporary roommate.

"Of course, you just have to know where to shop," Pat replies. I laugh, knowing we will never be shopping at the same places. "Well when you're the face of a new company, you have to look the part," he rationalizes.

I hold my hands up in surrender before snarking back, "Well half of the face. You have to deal with whatever Connor wants to wear. I guess it's lucky for you he can wear the hell out of jeans and a blazer."

"Haha, asshole. Yes I am only half of the new company. Hopefully we'll be putting Drew on display some as well. He really rounds us out into a more down-to-Earth crew."

Oh yes, I forgot Drew had joined the brewing company recently. "Head of marketing, right?" I ask.

"Yep, and so far he seems pretty happy. For the most part, at least. But I also have a feeling that having Lexa around will put him into a whole new orbit."

We both smile at the sentiment, thankful that we finally get to witness the Earth-shattering relationship that will be Drew and Lexa.

Thinking about them only draws my thoughts back to Grace again, though. I breathe out a small huff, not wanting to alert Patrick to my warring thoughts. He seems attuned to my mood, however, as his brows draw together in worry. I smile and say, "You want some of this coffee, I needed a caffeine fix."

He releases his face into a more relaxed position before replying, "Sure dude, thanks."

Chapter 7

Grace

"I heard the movie was pretty good last night," I say, giving Amanda a once-over. She looks radiant this morning. She's gotten a gorgeous tan and has a huge smile stretching her face. I'm still so thankful we connected last year at Ansley's wedding. Amanda quickly became one of my good friends and we talk all the time.

"Um, yeah it was great," she says, blushing. I can tell she's not just talking about the movie, but I am definitely not pushing for any details. Due to my weird feelings for my current travel buddy, I am not going to be digging into anyone else's romantic lives anytime soon. Not to say I was surprised about Drew dipping Lexa into a jaw-dropping kiss on the boat dock yesterday. We all saw that one coming.

We smile at each other over the rims of our cups, both obviously wanting to ask a personal question and shying away. I let my gaze fall back to my coffee, and release my thoughts back to last night.

The close call with Wes caused my dreams to go haywire. I've had some spicy dreams about him before, but they've always been rather vague. Having his hands on me and his mouth so close to mine inspired some rather heated moments in my imagination. I blush now, just thinking about it.

"Well, I need to run and get ready!" Amanda says, jumping up from her seat and setting her cup in the sink.

I watch as she makes her way over the threshold, wondering what she'll be wearing today. I haven't decided if it's a linen shorts and tank or sundress kind of day just yet. I'll have to try on a few outfits I think.

I take my last sip of coffee and sigh, thinking I should be able to just put on clothes without having to change so many times. Alas, I have yet to break myself of this habit in 29 years. *Maybe by 30*, I think, knowing it's unlikely.

I sigh again, wandering back to my room. I pull out the yellow sundress that I love as well as my white linen shorts and fitted green macrame top.

I feel like the sundress just looks like summer incarnate whereas the shorts and top look like island wear. I try on my island outfit first, turning this way and that in the mirror. *Those shorts might be a little too short*, I hear my mother's voice in my head. I wish I could rid myself of that voice sometimes. Don't get me wrong, I love my mother, we just butt heads often. Usually over my choice of clothing or who I'm seeing or my career....really just anything that doesn't align with how she wants me to live.

My parents are each other's one true love and it shows in the way they look at each other. I grew up with an amazing example of marriage, and I'm very thankful for that. My father is Spanish and embodies that to the fullest. Growing up, it was his way or the highway, but I always at least tried to choose his way. I respect the hell out of my parents and I would pretty much do anything they ask of me. Except wear calf length skirts and high collared shirts. That's where I draw the line.

With that thought in mind, I twirl in the mirror one more time and settle my mind. I love how these shorts look on my legs and the emerald green of this shirt is striking with my black hair. So onto shoes. And only one outfit tried on! It's a miracle.

Slipping into my favorite brown sandals, I make my way back into the kitchen. I see Amanda standing at the island counter, dressed in a pretty light yellow dress and I'm glad I stuck with my current outfit. She is a knockout. I smile and tell her so, to which she just scoffs and gestures at me with her hands.

"What?" I laugh.

"Just you! You are a living, breathing goddess. I am privileged to be allowed in your presence," she replies, and freaking curtsies.

"Okay, I hate you," I say, giggling. "Come on, before we're late."

"Yes, my queen."

I smack her arm lightly but can't help the laugh that spills out.

We ease out of the villa and down the boardwalk arm in arm, still sporting huge smiles.

My smile freezes in place when I spot Weston talking with Jackson. He's wearing a tight tank top showing off every delicious inch of his bare and well-muscled arms as well as his toned chest and abs. I almost start salivating but my attention is thankfully captured by Claire spinning towards me with a huge grin stretching her face.

"Hey girls! Are y'all excited for exploring the sweet little shops and all the great tourist traps? I know I am ready to be weighed down with random knick knacks and a bunch of stuff I don't need," she says, bubbly as ever.

"How much coffee did you have this morning?" Ansley asks, walking over to our group.

"Never enough!" Claire says, eyes rounding into saucers.

"Hmm, I beg to differ," I reply, laughing. "How do you survive with that much caffeine in your system?"

"Nurse anesthetist school requires more caffeine than nursing school did and I drank at least 4 cups a day then," Claire answers, shrugging.

We just shake our heads and laugh, knowing we'll never talk Claire out of her coffee addiction.

"Well, we ready to pile onto the bus?" Landon asks the group.

"Aye, aye captain!" we shout in unison, earning a head shake from him.

As we trek to the bus stop, I feel a distinct electricity radiating from my unoccupied side. I glance over and notice Weston has walked up, near enough to touch but without any actual contact.

"Get some good sleep last night?" I ask, not really meeting his eyes.

"Had some crazy dreams, but other than that...," he trails off, studying my profile.

I feel a tug on my other arm and look back to Amanda. "Hey girl, I'm gonna sit with Pat, you okay?"

"Yes ma'am, I think I can find a friend to sit with," I say, not willing to stop my friend from exploring whatever is going on there. Patrick seems like a good guy and he seems to be really interested in Amanda.

"Need a travel buddy?" Weston says, drawing my eyes to his mouth. He pulls his lower lip between his teeth at that exact moment and I inhale rather sharply. *Dammit, he definitely noticed that.*

"Yes, actually. Are you volunteering for that position?" I ask, ripping my gaze away from his mouth and back to his eyes.

"I'd be honored," he says, smirking.

"Well let's go...buddy," I retort with a wink. I start walking towards the bus, not stopping to see if he's following. Once I step onto the bus, I pause momentarily and take a look around. This is not what I was expecting. The inside of the bus is more like an RV—there's bench seats with tables between as well as couches and bean bag chairs. This bus is amazing. I'm staring around long enough that I feel a big body crash into the back of mine. I'm teetering on my tiptoes until an arm snakes around my middle and pulls me back into a rock hard chest. The breath whooshes out of my lungs and I hear a deep chuckle in my ear. Shivers run up and down my spine as I hear, "You okay there, travel buddy?"

I try my best to pull away but Weston has an iron grip on me. I'm basically just squirming against him, not that he seems to mind—if the harsh breaths I can feel on my neck aren't being misread.

I still, realizing that I'm probably just making this situation worse. As soon as I relax, Weston does the same. I feel the muscles in his forearm uncoil as he slips his arm from my body.

"Anytime now, there's still people trying to load up behind us," he says, obviously making fun of me at this point.

I shoot him a mean look, but only receive another laugh in response. *Ugh, the nerve.*

I make it up into the bus fully–under my own power–and choose a bench seat across from Amanda and Patrick. I slide onto the upholstered bench and look down at the table separating us. There's a menu on the table top with drinks and snacks. This is definitely the coolest bus I have ever been on.

As I'm perusing the alcoholic offerings, I feel Weston slide in beside me. His thigh is bared by the near-indecent length of his shorts and that skin connects immediately with mine. I feel an instant electric pulse thrumming between us. I sneak a glance at my new neighbor, trying to determine if he can feel it. Judging by the furrowed brow and pursed lips, he's just as confused by the way our bodies are reacting to each other. We've been in close proximity for almost a year, why is this happening now? There must be some weird magic powers this island possesses. I'm sure as soon as we're back in our mundane routine in Nevada, all of these instinctual bodily reactions to each other will dissipate. *Hopefully.*

Chapter 8

Weston

Every time my leg brushes Grace's, I feel something like an electric shock. This is weird. But also...enjoyable? I know she can feel it, too—she keeps sneaking glances at me in between talking to Amanda and Pat. We're not even to our first stop on the shopping trip. This is going to be a long day.

As that thought runs across my mind, Grace turns fully towards me for the first time today. As her dark brown eyes search my face and finally settle on my own eyes, she asks, "Why are you thinking about taking a separate contract? Please enlighten me."

"Um," I start, ever the clever orator, "I was just thinking of heading back towards home or taking a permanent post somewhere that we've been that I liked. But I know you're not really into the whole settling into one spot for too long type of thing."

Grace's mouth pops open in surprise, and stays like that for long enough that Amanda says, "Hey friend, you looking for something to drink? Your mouth is gonna dry out like that."

Grace's head whips toward her friend as I chuckle. Which only earns me a dark look from both of the women. I turn to Patrick, looking for some kind of support. My would-be ally only shrugs and sips on his cocktail. *Thanks dude.*

I just shake my head, trying to clear it a bit. I'm not sure why Grace chose now to try to have this conversation, but it's thrown me off balance. Dropping my gaze, I eye my drink, glad I settled on a mimosa rather than a rum drink. I pick up my glass and take a few sips, trying to let the champagne bubbles do their work of clearing my muddled thoughts.

Patrick and Amanda are doing a wonderful job of keeping Grace's attention. I can hear her musical laughter piercing my inner turmoil. I turn towards the sound that I love, meeting Grace's eyes. I know people talk about the sparkle in people's eyes, but Grace has an entire galaxy. When she laughs—really laughs—her eyes darken to almost midnight black with the most beautiful array of stars you've ever seen. I can't bear to look away, so I continue to stare.

The sparkle dims slightly, but her irises darken even further as she inhales sharply. I'm not sure what she's reading from my face, but if it's my thoughts, I'm in trouble. I adore this woman.

And this is the real reason I'm wary about continuing to travel together. I'm afraid of what might happen now that I've really acknowledged my feelings for her and seen the way she reacts to my touch. I'm not ready to start something she's only too eager to finish.

The bus slows to a stop, pulling me out of my own head. I feel Grace lightly pushing against my arm. Or rather, she seems to be putting some effort into it but it feels like she's hardly trying.

"You need something there, buddy?" I ask, still trying to emphasize our relationship as travel companions only.

"Yeah, *buddy*, I'm trying to get you to move so I can get to shopping!" she says, once again shoving my arm. It only causes me to laugh, seeing how much effort she's expending to barely move my arm.

I wouldn't call Grace petite by any means, she's tall and lean. But I don't remember the last time she went to the gym with me. She just has one of those naturally graceful bodies that people envy. But right now, I'm betting she wishes that she hit the bench press a couple more times this year.

I laugh again, starting to edge out of the booth. I let her continue to push like she's actually moving me.

"Whoa there, tiger," I say, faking a fall out of the seat.

"Oh my gosh, Wes. You are too much," Grace says, stepping lithely from her seat and rolling her eyes at me.

We both laugh off the tension we felt surrounding us while sitting in the booth together. I already feel like I can breathe more normally with some space between us. Not to say I mind how my chest fills with flutters when she's near.

Chapter 9

Grace

I can't stop touching all of the products as I wander through the shop that is the first of many stops today. I love the feel of the smooth fabrics that make up the clothing and the roughness of the fibers woven into the rugs and pillows. I wish I hadn't packed so many clothes to come here, I could have bought everything I needed here and been able to carry it back home.

As I'm thinking about how many new shirts I could sneak into other peoples' luggage, I feel a hand slide onto my lower back. I don't have to turn around to know who it is. "You're thinking about trying to sneak that into my bag aren't you?" Weston asks, leaving his hand on my back.

"How did you know?" I question, turning to him with widened eyes.

"I've been traveling with you for a year. You buy new things in every port and I know for a fact you don't have enough room in your bag to carry much back."

I duck my head, unwilling to admit how well Wes knows me. Before I have a chance to respond, he slips away, a small smile on his face.

"Oh that top would be absolutely stunning on you," Lexa says, sauntering up to where I'm still holding the light pink cotton blouse. I blink, realizing I'm still standing in the same spot and lower my hands. I shake my head and look at my friend.

"You don't think so?" she asks, misreading my response.

"Oh? No it's not—I'm not—" I pause, taking a breath, "Sorry, what?"

"Are you okay?" Lex says, placing a hand on my shoulder and turning me to fully face her.

"Yeah, I'm fine. I'm just, I don't know, confused?" I respond, still unsure of where my head is at.

"About?"

"My own thoughts." I huff out a laugh but Lexa only frowns.

"Anything you want to talk about?" She runs her hand over my shoulder blades in a soothing gesture I remember from our days in nursing school. Lexa was always the first to comfort a friend, even before she started showing her full emotional side to us.

"No, really. I'm okay. I just need some more sleep, I think. Maybe some caffeine. Food. A new shirt," I laugh, holding up the top still in my hands.

"It really is cute. You should get it. That color looks so good on you. Well, every color looks good on you. It's hard not to get jealous over that fact. Especially with my creamy white complexion and red hair. There's some colors that make me look like a clown."

"I doubt that somehow," I say, pulling my sweet friend into a crushing hug. "You're way too fierce not to pull off anything you try on."

"I concur," Drew says, wrapping his long arms around both of us. "About both of you. I can't believe I'm surrounded by so many smart, funny and beautiful women. It must be some kind of Bermuda Triangle of friend groups."

"Oh, whatever," Lexa says, turning to smack Drew on the arm. They are honestly just the sweetest couple and getting to witness them finally come together has been nothing short of a miracle.

I smile and ease away, letting them have a moment. I love having friends that are willing to hug. I love hugs. And just touch in general. Definitely my love language.

I hang onto the shirt, deciding that I can squeeze one more item into my suitcase. As I make my way towards the register, I see a shelf of ceramics. It pulls me up short seeing all of the colorfully painted pots and plates. It takes me back to my earliest visits to my dad's childhood home in Spain. My grandparents used to love taking me to pottery classes and art shows. My family thought I was going to be some type of artist when I grew up due to my love for all things bright and my passion for creating. It confused my grandmother to no end when I went into nursing and chose to work in an ICU. When we FaceTime they still ask me if I've drawn or written anything new recently. I can feel the weight of their disappointment that I let my creativity "go to waste", as they say.

I let my fingers graze the lines and swirls of the paint on the plates and resist the urge to question my choices. I'm happy where I am. I love what I do and I love my patients. Working in critical care involves its own kind of creative process and it's an environment that I thrive in.

But as my thoughts are turning over, my eyes fall onto the most beautiful display of hand painted journals. My hands follow my eyes and I pick up a journal with a light blue cover, painted with a gorgeous sunset and *free your dreams* written in calligraphy across the bottom. It feels like a sign and one that I'm not willing to ignore.

I take the journal and the shirt to the front to pay, still lost in my head.

"Will this be all, dear?" the sweet cashier asks me.

"Yes ma'am," I respond.

I'm digging through my purse for my wallet when I see her hands slide into my peripheral vision. "Sure you don't need these as well?" she asks, pushing a set of colored pencils onto the stack. "They're free with a journal purchase." She smiles knowingly at me, like she can see that my hands are itching for some sort of creative outlet for my thoughts this week.

"Oh, okay then! Thank you," I say, finally meeting her eyes. It causes me to pause, hand still in my purse. She has the same exact eyes as my Grammy—my grandmother who passed away last year. Where the Spanish relatives on my dad's side are expectant, my Grammy only wanted me to dream and to follow those dreams. She always told me to listen to my head and heart. Well Grammy, that's what's causing the problem right now. My head and my heart are telling me two different things.

I come to my senses, pulling my payment from my bag and taking my new purchases. I don't run into anyone else from our group as I make my way out of the store, wanting to be alone with my new journal for a moment.

I find a bench, settle in and open the pages. They're a creamy color with a bit of texture. Without a conscious thought, I pull a colored pencil from the pack and start sketching. I'm not sure what I'm even drawing until a shape starts taking form. From the shadings on the page emerges a man's hand, thrust into the base of dark hair, the hair spilling over the clasping fingers. I inhale a sharp breath, realizing where my sketch is heading.

"Watcha doin?" I slam my notebook closed before looking up at the owner of the hand in my sketch. I blush furiously, unable to speak for a moment.

Once I regain the ability to form words, I say, "Oh, um just sketching."

"Yeah? I didn't know that you drew," Weston says, trying to take a peek at the page.

"I don't! Or at least not anymore, not for a while. I just saw this notebook and it felt like it was calling to me. I was thinking it might be nice to start sketching again. Nothing too crazy." I start loading my book and pencils back into my bag, getting ready to stand and make my way back onto the bus.

Chapter 10

Grace

We're given a sudden reprieve from the heat as we settle into our seats. The A/C is blasting on here and I am so thankful for it. Amanda slides in across from me, huge smile on her face.

"What did you find, darling?" I ask, clearing the table so she can spread out her loot. Amanda is a compulsive shopper and I live for her hauls.

"Well...," she starts, pulling an adorable stuffed iguana, "I'll never forget watching Lexa climb Landon like a tree to get away from that cute little guy on the trail yesterday." We all laugh, watching as Lex blushes from the memory.

The bag in her lap continues to lighten as she unloads a set of ceramic bowls painted with island scenes, a small snow globe because apparently her mom collects them and finally, a blanket woven from the fibers of the palm leaves and coconuts.

"Where are you going to put all of that stuff on the flight back?" I ask, genuinely worried about her charges for her bag being overweight.

"Oh! I always pack a collapsible carry-on in my luggage for

the stuff I buy on trips!" she replies, proud of her forethought. That is actually a very good idea. Maybe I can find a cute bag or backpack here to carry my stuff home in.

Patrick captures Amanda's attention and they settle into a conversation concerning her mother's snow globe collection.

"Did you end up buying that top?" Weston asks, nudging my arm with his elbow.

"I did, actually. I couldn't pass it up once I felt the fabric," I reply with a smile.

"It's going to look amazing on you. That's not surprising though, considering everything looks good on you."

A blush rushes across my cheeks, making me drop my gaze from Weston's face.

"Hey," he says, using his thumb and forefinger to raise my face back up to his, "You are gorgeous and you need to get used to people telling you that."

"Yeah? Because you plan on saying it all the time now?" I ask, trying—and failing—to remove my chin from his grasp.

"If you'll let me," he whispers. I finally pull my face away from him and look to see that Amanda and Patrick are staring at us.

"Everything...okay?" Patrick asks, looking between me and Weston.

"Yes, it's fine. Everything is fine," I rush out, pasting a smile on my lips.

They seem to let it go, sliding back into their conversation and leaving us to sort out whatever is happening.

"It changed things for me," I feel his breath whisper close to my ear.

I shudder, knowing exactly what he's talking about, but not willing to admit to my own feelings having changed.

≫→

The rest of the day goes about the same, the group traipsing in and out of shops and places to eat. We've eaten so many delectable things today and I am stuffed. I can't imagine eating anything else when our driver drops us off at our last location of the evening. The smells emanating from the restaurant ahead of me make my stomach roar with excitement. *I guess I do have some more room in there,* I reason.

We walk into the open air space and I am immediately bombarded with the scent of roasting lamb and spiced honey. My mouth is watering by the time we make it to our table. Apparently our tour came with ready-made reservations to this amazing eatery.

Once seated, we order a round of champagne to start off our night. This is the last night of our vacation and we're celebrating. I love this group so much.

As the night passes, we have several more glasses of champagne along with a round of rum and cokes to have a last taste of the island's famous spirit.

"So, what's going on with you and Weston?" Lexa asks, leaning into my side.

"What do you mean?" I deflect.

"You know what I mean. I've seen the looks y'all have been throwing this week."

"I think you're just seeing love everywhere now that you've finally admitted yours," I reply with a wink.

"You're probably not wrong," she says, shrugging.

"Nothing, though. To answer your question—there's nothing happening. Nothing has and I don't think anything will."

"Are you *wanting* something to happen?" she asks, staring into my soul.

"Um...I really don't know. I don't know what I want or what I'm feeling." I show her my emotions, letting her take a turn at deciphering what I can't.

Chapter 11

Weston

The rest of our island trip ended up being pretty uneventful. We boarded a small plane that took us back to Miami and from there Grace and I loaded up to head back to Nevada. We had a layover in Houston which was nice. I can't stand to be on a flight longer than five hours.

We've been back in Reno for about two weeks now, getting settled back into our rhythm of working and sleeping. We work opposite shifts which makes it easier for us both to sleep but harder for us to have any time to interact.

I thought there would be a change in our behavior towards each other once we got back and it was just the two of us, but that hasn't seemed to be the case. At least not yet. We've been sleeping and working too much to really have time to even discuss what almost happened in St. Croix.

Grace and I are both off for the weekend and after she sleeps through the day, I think we have plans to hang out tonight. At least takeout dinner and a stupid horror flick. Like I said, we're right back in our rhythm.

I can't even begin to explain how much I hate it.

I am so on edge every time I come home. I just want to be able to get in from work, scoop Grace up into my arms and carry her to bed. Even if it's just to sleep. I can't help but remember the way she looked at me when our mouths were so close we were breathing the same air. She wanted me, but I don't know if she's willing to admit that to herself.

Grace has been very distant since we got back, not unfriendly, just roommate-like. She avoids any circumstances in which we might have to touch. She doesn't even look in my direction when I leave my room sometimes. I notice she glances at me out of the side of her eye and only gives me her full attention when I'm wearing a shirt. I realized pretty early on in the week that I was making her uncomfortable in any state of undress. So as warm as it is, I wear a shirt and sweatpants around almost 24/7 now. The last thing I want is to cause her any distress. Which is why I also haven't reminded her of the almost-kiss or attempted to even get close to her.

This all makes me a little nervous about movie night, though. Our normal TV-watching positions include her feet in my lap or her head on my shoulder depending on the type of movie. Scary movies usually make her even more inclined to be close to me.

Regardless, we'll be hanging out and hopefully having a conversation that doesn't revolve around work.

Grace is still asleep, having worked last night, so I'm heading out to the gym so she has quiet in the apartment. I grab my headphones and my laptop so I can head to a coffee shop after I work out. Nothing like a non-fat iced latte to cool you down after a good sweat.

⇻

I spend more time at the gym than usual, still trying to work off those vacation carbs. Once I feel like I've gotten a good amount of work in, I head to the showers to rid myself of my stink. I would hate to smell up the coffee shop.

In no time, I'm strolling into the shop, inhaling the vibrant scent of roasting coffee and vanilla. This place is great, though still not as good as the place Drew took me to back in Savannah the last time I was in town.

I place my order and settle into a table in the back, connect my laptop to the WiFi and pull up my game. I don't get to play as often as I'd like, but there was also a time in my life that I was obsessed with video games. Growing up with four older sisters, it was something I could do on my own that they weren't all necessarily interested in. Kiera, the one that's closest to my age, would play certain games with me. We're still close and I can't play Super Smash Bros without thinking of her.

As if I conjured her with my thoughts alone, my phone starts ringing with a FaceTime call from Kiera.

"Well hello, sis. What's up?" I answer, giving her a smile that I reserve just for her.

"Well, my darling little brother, I have a question for you," she replies, somewhat cryptically.

"I probably have an answer…"

"Well, so you know the wedding is in a couple of months? The middle of September?" she asks.

"Whose wedding?" I ask, laughing when she gasps in shock. "Kee, you know I'm kidding. What are you wanting to ask me? If I'll be your ring bearer?"

She rolls her eyes, but finally gets to the point. "I know you already have a few responsibilities, but would you walk me down the aisle?"

I tear up slightly, but answer, "Yes, of course. I would love to. What an honor." I can't say much more than that without full-on sobbing. It brings me back to the day that Kiera called me to tell me about the engagement last year.

I answer her call like I always do, with a huge smile on my face. I can't imagine being happier than when I get to talk to my sisters.

That thought is proven wrong when in the next moment—and without a word—Kee flips her hand up to the screen, showing off a new piece of hardware on her ring finger.

My smile grows impossibly wider as I whisper-shout, "Kiera, oh my God! I can't believe Nick finally lost his mind and popped the question!"

I'm rewarded with pursed lips and a glare before my sister responds, "Okay you big oaf. I was happy with your excitement there for a second. I should have known better."

"Kee, you know I'm excited and so happy for you and for Nick. You two have been together long enough that he definitely knows what he's getting into."

"I know right? Apparently that's what mom told him when he asked her permission."

I laugh a bit before sobering at the next thought that crosses my mind. Nick asked our mom because our dad wasn't around to give his blessing. With his passing a few years ago, this has been a continuous process of realizing all of the things he's missing. He walked two of my sisters down the aisle but won't be here for Kiera's wedding. Or Tessa's. Or mine, if I'm ever lucky enough to find someone.

"You know Dad loved Nick, just like the rest of us," I say, wanting to remind Kiera that he's still here with us, in our hearts and minds.

"I know. Or he wouldn't have gotten to come back after dropping me off late for curfew on our third date."

Kiera and Nick have been together since high school. They were wanting to tie the knot a couple of summers ago, but Nick had told me he didn't feel right still proposing when we had just lost our father. I think Kiera was thankful for the reprieve at first, but it did cause a bit of a problem that he continued to wait.

They have been living together since she graduated from law school about 4 years ago now. I know she's over-the-moon excited about the engagement.

I'm brought back to the present hearing Kiera's voice coming through my speakers now.

"I knew you'd be alone, not doing anything and ready to talk," she laughs.

"For your information, I am not alone. I am in a crowded coffee house. About to engage in some well-simulated elf battles. So there," I say in my defense.

"Mkay, little bro. Whatever you say. Have you locked it down with your way-too-good-for-you roommate yet?"

I roll my eyes and say something I can't even believe comes out of my mouth, "Actually yes. We're together. Happy?"

I have no idea why I just said that. Why did I tell Kiera that Grace and I are dating? We're very much not dating. Whatever the opposite of dating is, that's what we're doing. *What is wrong with me?*

"Happy? I'm ecstatic! She can be your date to the wedding!"

"Oh um, she might be busy. I'll check," I stutter, like I don't know we're going to be in the same place and in Oregon. We just signed the paperwork with our agency.

"I'm a planner, what can I say? Well, just let me know if you'll be bringing her to the rehearsal dinner as well, okay?" Kiera says, already writing Grace on the guest list.

Chapter 12

Weston

I arrive back at the apartment just in time to see Grace stumbling out of her room and into the kitchen.

"Hey, sleepyhead. I brought you some coffee from JoJo's," I say, lifting up the second cup. Grace squints her eyes in my direction before shuffling towards me and the coffee I know she's craving.

"Thanks," I hear, grumbled from under her breath. It takes Grace a minute to wake up, whether it's morning or night. I wait patiently, letting the warm caffeine make its way into her system.

Once I see the light entering her eyes I say, "Guess what!"

I watch as she jerks back slightly, affronted by my enthusiasm while she's still trying to adjust to being vertical. "What?" she asks, almost deadpan.

"Kiera called me while I was at the coffee shop and asked me to walk her down the aisle," I continue.

"Aww Wes, that is so sweet. You almost cried, didn't you?" she asks, smile coming through fully now.

"It was close," I reply, grinning. As an intended side note I rush out, "Oh and they all think we're dating now and you're supposed to come to the wedding with me. Do you want me to go ahead and order the Thai food or are you not hungry yet?"

"Wait, wait, wait, go back. What?" she stutters, shaking her head like she still needs to clear the cobwebs.

"Are you ready to eat? I can go ahead and order the food–" I begin.

"No Weston. You know that's not the part I'm asking about."

"Oh, um, well, so...," I say, unable to get this out, "I, um, accidentally said we were together. When she asked. If we were together. I'm not sure why."

"You can still correct that. You have like a year to correct that. We can fake break up between now and then," she says, fire entering her dark brown eyes.

"Well, so the wedding is mid–September. During the next contract. That we already signed together," I say, unable to make full eye contact with Grace now that I'm pretty sure she's trying to literally kill me with her glare.

"So let me get this straight. You want me to go to a wedding with you in a few months, acting like I'm your girlfriend. And I can't get out of this at all because I'm now forced to spend the next couple of months living with you. Again. Why Weston? Why would you tell your sister we were dating? She's seen us together a lot over the last year. If we're not actually dating, she's going to know and it's going to be awkward."

"Well, there's an obvious solution here...," I hedge, catching my bottom lip between my teeth and looking at her from between my lashes.

"Yeah? You admitting to Kiera that you lied?" she asks.

"Or actually dating?" I respond. Smiling like it's not the

stupidest thing I've said in my adult life.

"Alright. I'm going to act like you didn't just say that. Let's just...forget this conversation for now. Maybe I'll go back to bed and wake back up and this was all a nightmare."

"It would be a nightmare to date me?" I ask, genuinely affronted.

"No Wes–that's not–ugh. Let me finish my coffee. Then we'll order food and sit down and talk okay? I need the full dose of caffeine and some food for this," she says, huffing and moving towards the living room.

It takes me a moment to catch up to what she's doing, but as I finally follow her into the room, I see our streaming service pulled up on the TV.

"What are you wanting to watch? It's horror night, right?" she asks me aloud. Under her breath I hear her mumble, "Sure feels like it."

What the hell? I knew she wasn't into having a full-blown relationship right now, I just didn't realize that she was so against one with me. Maybe I misread all of those signals in St. Croix. I guess I was the only one falling this whole time.

As I settle onto the far end of the couch I wonder, who will be there to catch me when I hit the ground?

Chapter 13

Grace

What was he thinking? Why would he tell his sister we were dating? Does he really think a near-kiss on an island on vacation equals a relationship? He hasn't even made another move towards me since we've been back.

To be fair, I haven't really made myself available for such an endeavor. I've been avoiding him. Avoiding being alone with him, seeing him shirtless and any situation where we're close enough for me to mess up again.

Because that's what happened that night in St. Croix. I messed up. I was willing to give myself fully to Weston and he wasn't ready at all to accept my offer. We're in different places right now. As evidenced by the fact that he so casually mentioned us just *dating for real* like I don't have other options. Like I'm just sitting around, waiting for him to notice that I want to be with him. Like—I am. That's exactly what I'm doing. I'm playing hard to get without having given him any inclination that I'm actually interested.

Maybe I could change that tonight. We already have a long

conversation ahead of us. I could bargain a bit. He gets his wedding date and I get...what? Him? I'll have to mull this over with noodles.

➣➝

Noodles in hand, movie playing, I let silence settle over us as I contemplate the discussion we'll soon be having. If we're going to act like we're dating, we're going to probably have to kiss in front of his family. And I really don't want our first kiss to happen at the rehearsal dinner. So we could just...practice? I guess?

This film isn't nearly as terrifying as the critics made it out to be. I can sense Weston's attention wavering just as much as mine. I reach down to grab the remote, ready to pause the movie so we can go ahead and talk. Wes must have the same thought because his hand grabs mine as I wrap my fingers around the plastic. A jolt of electricity pulses through my fingers and I drop the remote instantly.

Wes looks up at me, eyes rounded in shock, "You okay? I was just going to pause the movie."

"Yeah–I just–sorry. I was thinking the same thing. Want to talk?" I ask, still attempting to rein in my breathing.

"Yeah, now is as good a time as any I suppose," he says, turning towards me fully on the couch.

As I scoot my legs around to face him, our knees brush, sending another shock through me. I shiver but maintain eye contact, trying to hold onto the courage that led me to this moment.

"So, what do I get out of this arrangement?" I ask, quirking a brow.

"Well, free alcohol and a chance to party with my sisters?" Weston suggests.

"You're gonna have to do better than that," I counter.

"Um...I'll...pay for your dress?"

"And new shoes?" I ask.

"And new shoes, of course," he relents.

I stick my hand out, waiting for him to shake and make our deal official. He stares at my outstretched hand for a while before making a move towards it. Hesitant, like it's a snake about to strike. Before making contact, however, he pulls his hand sharply back, looking back up at me and into my eyes.

"No other stipulations? What about the whole, ya know, having to act like my girlfriend?" he asks, obviously worried that I'm prepared to back out at any point.

"Well, as far as *that* is concerned, my only suggestion is that we maybe get the physical stuff out of the way before your family has to witness the most awkward first kiss in history," I reply, as nonchalantly as possible—with my heart pounding in my chest. What if he refuses this part? I'll have to act like the doting girlfriend to someone who won't even kiss me.

"Physical—out of the—kiss—wait what?" Weston's voice breaks slightly throughout the external processing of my statement.

"You know, like practice kissing and hand holding and touching so it doesn't look forced or as fake as it's going to be. Or would you rather blow your cover right out of the gate?" I ask, throwing out my extended hand in exasperation.

"Well no, obviously not. But what you're talking about sounds mostly like friends with benefits. Is that what you're saying?"

"Sure, we can go with that. Whatever works so that we don't embarrass ourselves at this wedding." I shrug, starting to pull my hand back in. It seems like this might be the deal breaker for Wes.

Weston seems to contemplate for a moment, eyes scrunching and forehead furrowing, before coming to a conclusion. He smiles, stretches his hand out and says, "Deal. Friends with benefits to practice for the wedding."

I balk at how well he's taking this, having assumed this would be far out of his comfort zone. Weston is definitely a relationship guy. I'm almost concerned about why he's agreeing to this until I remember that he's the one that got us into this situation by lying to Kiera.

"Deal," I finally repeat. And just like the last several times, as soon as our hands meet, my skin tingles with the electricity running between us.

I intake a sharp breath and blink up at Weston. "When do we get started?" he asks, voice rumbling low.

"Well, I guess whenever. I got plenty of sleep today, so we can go ahead and start work-shopping the kissing I guess?" I suggest, still unsure of how this is going to really work.

"Workshop?" he laughs. "Should we also brainstorm places to touch each other in a loving way and strategize hand holding?"

I scoff, but he's right. I can't keep acting like this is a group project from school. This is emotions and feelings and maybe, passion. "You know what I mean." I blanch, remembering that I just had smelly Asian food and clap my hand over my mouth. "Can I go brush my teeth first?"

"Of course, what's kissing if not a planned act that everyone needs to have their best hygiene to perform?"

I roll my eyes, but get up from the couch. I turn to tell him that maybe he could follow suit, but he's not looking at my face. His eyes are firmly attached to my ass, mostly visible due to the small shorts that I sleep in. It takes him a moment to realize that said ass is no longer moving and his eyes snap back to mine. I quirk my brow in question.

"Hurry back," he says, all heat and smoke. I shiver but turn back towards my original destination.

Oh no, I'm in trouble.

Chapter 14

Weston

I cannot believe this is happening. Grace is out of her mind if she thinks all I'm planning on doing is kissing practice. She didn't lay out any terms for what our new relationship will entail. I plan to take this as far as she'll let me. I can't go too fast though. I know she caught me staring at her ass as she was leaving the room, but I've been waiting for that opportunity for months now. She always wears those tiny shorts to bed and I—being the gentleman that I am—have kindly averted my gaze, as much as possible anyway. But now that she's agreed to this arrangement, it's game on.

She takes my advice and hurries back from the bathroom. It's adorable that she's worried about her breath when it's taking everything in my power just to keep my hands to myself.

If I can behave tonight, I think I have a strong chance of doing the impossible. Once she sees how good of a *fake* boyfriend I am, she won't be able to resist having the real thing. Little does she know, this is as real as it gets for me.

Grace takes her time arranging her long, lean legs back

underneath her on the couch. She tucks herself back under her blanket and gently lays her hands on top of her lap, Then she just sits there, staring at me expectantly. "So...is this what I hurried back for? To be stared at as you lick your lips like I'm your next meal?"

Oh, honey, it's like you can read my mind. "I'm letting you get settled in. I'm nothing if not patient."

"Mmm," she hums, causing her vocal chords to tighten in her throat. My eyes are drawn to the long column of her neck and I am near salivating, thinking of the taste of her skin. *All in good time.*

I'm having a harder and harder time not making a lunge for her, when suddenly she darts forward. As graceful as she looks, she is anything but in this moment. Her foot gets caught in the blanket and her hand stretches out to steady herself. Unfortunately for her, it lands right on my crotch. I suck in a sharp breath and reach down, circling my hand around her wrist, pulling her away and up towards my face. I take in full and rounded lips in the second before I let my eyes drift closed, our lips touching for the first time. When people talk about fireworks, I don't know if they've experienced anything like this. There is a physical shock as our mouths meet that rattles me to my core. I groan, pulling her even tighter to me. I snake my hand into her hair, using the leverage to hold her in place. Our mouths are moving in tandem, tongues darting out to explore each other's lips. This is at once the most timid and the most explosive kiss I have ever experienced. I am immediately intoxicated and it is almost painful to pull back, but I do. I use my grip on her to pull her back as I release a shaky breath. We're both panting, eyes wild and searching.

Oh shit, we're in trouble.

"Okay well, I'm going to my room, to uh, read. Or something," Grace rushes out, trying to stand. Her feet are still tangled up in the blanket and she stumbles again. I reach out my hand to steady her and feel that now-familiar tingle when our skin meets. She shoots me a look and then takes off to her room.

Well that was weird. I'm tempted to give her the space she's requesting, but an overwhelming need to check in on her arises. I need to make sure she's okay and not uncomfortable.

I stand from the couch, taking a deep breath and running a hand through my hair. That was intense and I'm stunned by the heat I felt pouring from her. I was so sure that I had mistaken what I saw in St. Croix.

As I walk towards Grace's closed door, I can hear sounds coming from her room that I can't decipher. There's a shuffling noise, along with clipped breathing and possibly like a razor? I'm not sure, there's some kind of buzzing.

I raise my hand and knock, "You okay? Do you need to talk or anything?" Whatever was happening before is not happening now. There are loud crashes and stuttered curses and the buzzing stops.

"No, I'm okay! Sorry, we'll talk in the morning! So tired. Goodnight!" she says, her voice muffled by the door between us.

I stand there for a minute more, still unsure of what I need to be doing, before I walk back to the living room. I plop back down on the couch, pick up the remote and as I'm turning the movie back on, it hits me. The buzzing, the breathing, the shuffling–Grace wasn't–*was she?*

Chapter 15

Grace

Not one of my finer moments by far. As I listen to Weston's footsteps retreating from my door, I take a deep breath and focus on the ceiling for a minute. I was not expecting him to follow me to my room, he's never done that before. But I guess we've never kissed before either. And damn, what a first kiss that was.

I had to run to my room, knowing I wasn't going to get what I needed from Wes tonight. I'm sure kissing me was too much for him. Let alone helping me get a release. There's been so much tension built up in me since St. Croix and that searing kiss lit a fuse. I was close when Weston knocked, causing me to throw my favorite little battery-operated toy into my nightstand like I was hiding a spicy book from my mom. Embarrassment has flooded it's way through my body. There's no way Weston didn't know what was going on in here.

I continue to stare at the ceiling, even more frustrated than before. It's not like this is the first time Weston has popped into my head while I've been trying to relieve some stress. This is the first time, however, that I could vividly picture how his hands feel on me and how he tastes. He kisses like he wants to consume me.

I groan, thrashing on the bed like a toddler throwing a tantrum. How stupid am I to be attracted to my roommate who has never made any type of advance towards me? He probably still just thinks of me as a friend who has now asked him to do something weird in exchange for what really just amounts to a big favor. I've met most of his family before, acting like I'm his girlfriend shouldn't be that hard, right?

But if he tries to kiss me like that in front of them, I will turn into a puddle of goo. We're going to have to keep practicing so I can learn to not be so affected.

It's been a week since the kiss. We had a weekend off together in which I could barely look at Weston following the incident outside of my room. But it hasn't been unpleasant in the apartment. In between working, I've been noticing he's doing small things for me—making coffee before I get up for work, adding shows to our watch list that he thinks I'll like and putting my book on the coffee table when he finds it in random places like the cabinets.

I guess he's trying to get in my good graces, considering the whole wedding date issue. He probably thinks I'm more upset about it than I am. But if it gets me coffee and good shows, I'll let him think that as long as he needs to.

We're both off again today, so we're planning on heading to a place nearby with some new friends to grab some Sunday brunch. I pick my outfit more carefully than I normally would, taking care to wear the new top from St. Croix that Weston liked.

I'm hoping a few mimosas will give me enough courage to broach the topic of more kissing practice. This is our last week in Reno, then we have a week to make it to Marion County, Oregon.

The car ride to the brunch spot is quiet. I don't know if we're both tired or if we're both nervous of being around our friends together after everything that's happened recently. If I was a betting woman, it would be the latter. I'm banking on the fact that our friends here haven't seen enough of us together to know if we're acting weird.

As we pull up to the restaurant, I remain immobile long enough that Weston walks around the car and to my door. He gently opens it, bending over to look me in the eye. "You okay there, buddy?" he asks.

I let my eyes linger on his lips longer than necessary until I finally reply, "Yep, I'm great. I was just in my head a bit there."

"Yeah I noticed. Anything you want to talk about before we head in there?" he asks, still invading my space in the most comfortable way.

I swing my legs to the side, attempting to get out of the car. Weston doesn't move an inch, causing me to be pressed right up against his body as I try to rise out of the vehicle. My chest is heaving, trying to intake a breath with no air. I feel like I'm suffocating, while my heart is still beating out of my chest. I could die right here, and honestly not be that upset about it. Enveloped in the heat of this large male body, lashes fluttering like a preteen, and not even embarrassed about it.

I watch as Weston's lips curve into a smile that melts me even further. With one hand on the door and the other on top of the car, he's caging me in and he knows it. Still, he doesn't make a move to let me out. Just as I feel like I could pass out from lack of air, he takes a step back. Then another, and another, until he's far enough that I can actually stand without fear of toppling back into the seat.

"You gonna just stand there?" I ask with more confidence than I'm feeling. "I'm starving and would like to eat something soon."

"Yes ma'am. Lead the way," he croons, stepping aside slightly and gesturing forward.

As I take a step past him, I feel a large hand rest on my lower back. I'm tempted to snap my head around, but I have to get used to touches like this if we're going to prove to his family that we're dating. I try to relax into the touch, not wanting Weston to feel the tension under his palm. I was the one that suggested this part of the arrangement, the least I could do is not freak out every time we touch. It's hard, though, with that electrical current that we still have running underneath our skin. I would swear it was built up static if we weren't on concrete right now. It was easy enough to play off at the apartment, in the dark. But in the light of day—in public—it's hard to act unaffected.

I finally do turn to look at Weston, but his eyes are straight ahead. He has a sweet, small smile on his lips and when he sees me looking at him, he uses his thumb to trace a pattern on my lower back. I smile, feeling reassured already. As much as his touch can unsettle me one moment, it's a great source of comfort in the next.

I take a deep breath, settling my nerves and looking forward to brunch.

As soon as we're inside the restaurant I hear, "Gracie!!" shouted from several mouths. I whip my head towards the sound, huge smile overtaking my face as I see my work friends.

Kimmy, Melinda and Bruce are all here from the ICU. Weston invited Freddy and Dan who are both sitting opposite my buds. We've made friends at every hospital we've been at so far and I have loved keeping in touch with all of them.

With our friends surrounding us, I immediately forget any uneasiness I felt in the parking lot. I let go and just enjoy my time with people I love.

Chapter 16

Weston

I love seeing Grace around friends. She comes alive in a way that is so wholly her. Her face lights up, her smile is easy and her laughter is contagious. Where she seemed a little uncomfortable in the car, she is fully immersed in the conversation now. She's one of those friends that remembers everything you've ever told her.

"Bruce, how is your little niece? She's what, 6 months now?" Grace asks, causing Bruce to break into a huge smile and launch into tales of his niece that has everyone laughing.

"You okay, man? You're more quiet than normal," Dan says, elbowing me in the ribs to get my attention.

"Huh? Oh yeah, I'm fine. Just in my head, I guess," I reply, giving my full attention to him.

"In your head, or in your new relationship?" he asks, glancing pointedly towards my arm slung casually over Grace's chair.

"Oh, we're not together. We're just friends, for now," I say, dropping my voice for the last part.

Dan only hitches his brow at me, skeptical but willing to let it go.

I know that Grace is nowhere near feeling how I do, but she'll get there. I'm sure of it.

The rest of our brunch is filled with stories of funny hospital exploits, reminders to please come back and visit once we leave in a few weeks and an invitation to spend the 4th of July on Kimmy's boat. Grace and I both work the beginning of the week, but it would be nice to spend the holiday with our friends before we move the next week.

"What do you say? Boat day?" I ask Grace, dropping my hand to squeeze her shoulder.

She gives a slight shiver that only I notice, but answers, "Absolutely! That sounds perfect Kim! Thank you!"

We say our goodbyes and I watch as Grace hugs everyone, somewhat jealous of her willingness to give them casual contact when ours basically has to be planned out. I keep a smile on my face though, willing to play this game as long as possible if I can be with Grace in the end.

On our way back to the apartment, it's silent again. But, the silence is filled with a buzzing tension that was not noticeable on the way there. I look at Grace several times, just to see her staring out the window and fiddling her hands in her lap. As we near home, I reach over to touch her hands, wanting to stop her from tearing at the skin around her nails like I've seen her do before.

As my hand brushes her, she gasps and turns toward me. There's so much heat in her dark brown eyes, they're almost black. It takes effort to rip my eyes away, afraid I'll wreck the car if I keep staring. It's only then that I realize she's still clasping onto my hand that I left in her lap.

Grace starts drawing shapes on my palm with her fingers, causing tingles to run up my arm and down into my core. I am not going to make it home if she keeps this up. I throw the car into park as soon as we're back at the apartment and shift in my seat until I'm facing her.

"Want to get some more practice in this afternoon?" she asks, eyes hooded and a small smirk on her lips.

"Sounds like a plan," comes my stilted reply. "Inside right? If you keep it up with your fingers there, it might be happening right here."

I watch her throat as she swallows her next breath. She just nods and releases my hand, much to my eternal disappointment. I stifle the grimace forming, knowing that I get to kiss her as soon as we're upstairs.

The elevator ride to our apartment is one of the longest 30 second spans of my life. You could cut the tension with a knife and my hands are itching to touch her. I can tell that she notices because she's fidgeting and inching closer and closer to me. The bell dings and the door slides open—finally. I watch as she slides the key in the door with trembling hands.

The door opens and I crowd her inside, slamming it closed behind me. I spin her around, putting her back up against the door. I pull the clip from her hair, releasing her dark curls and running my fingers through it until I can grasp the base. Her mouth parts and I steal her next breath.

The sparks are flying so fast, I'm afraid I'm going to be consumed by her fire. She presses her body against mine, fisting her hands in my shirt to pull me closer. I let my other hand fall to her hip, then slide down the back of her leg, lifting her off the floor. She instinctively wraps her legs around my hips and I deepen the kiss with a groan. I run my tongue along her lips, asking for permission which she grants. The second our tongues touch, it's over for me. I'm lost in this moment and I never want to come back. She groans into my mouth as her hands move from my shirt to wrap around my neck. She starts running her fingers through the short hair at the base of my skull and I swear I am about to start purring. I've never felt a kiss like this before. This is magical.

Chapter 17

Grace

This is so good it's almost painful. Knowing that this is something I can't have forever has me wishing I wouldn't have instigated this today. Weston is absolutely devouring me, body and soul, and I don't want it to end. But this is going way beyond practice.

I know that I need to stop this, but I'm powerless to. As I continue to run my fingers through his hair, he breaks the kiss long enough to say, "I really like this top, by the way." I suck in a quick breath, knowing that I won't be able to breathe again in a moment. I use my hands on his neck to pull him back into me. He has me fully pressed up against the door, taking any other form of control away from me.

I feel my back peel away from the door and my eyes fly open, worried that I'm falling or that he's stopping—I can't tell which would be worse.

He pulls away again, only to smirk at me as he walks us over to the kitchen island. He sets me down, my eyes above his now that I'm sitting. He looks up at me from under his lashes, then drops his gaze back down to the aforementioned blouse. His hands drift from my waist up to the back of my neck. He begins untying the halter of the shirt, arching a brow in question. I can only nod my consent and I draw my bottom lip in between my teeth.

"Hey, quit that. The only teeth that lip should be between are mine," he says, voice husky and so sexy.

"Yes sir," I smirk, letting my lip pop back out and running my tongue along it. His eyes are firmly fixed on my mouth now and I use that to my advantage. I grip the back of his head and bring his lips back to mine. He groans loudly, finally untying my shirt from around my neck and my back. The cotton material drops off my body and he pulls me to the edge of the counter. His hands are just as thorough as his mouth has been, leaving no part of me untouched.

My hands slide from his hair, down his shoulders and to the buttons on the front of his shirt. I deftly flick each button open, baring his chest to me. Sliding the shirt off of his shoulders, I can't keep my hands from running over his impressive arm muscles. My fingers tease over his pecs and then down to his stomach. He shivers in response to my touch, but doesn't stop me. He just continues feasting on my mouth and swallowing my breath. He is consuming me.

Just as I think I might die from lack of oxygen, he breaks the kiss and takes a step back. I feel chilled, though I'm burning like an inferno. I realize I'm panting and holding onto his waistband for dear life. His gaze travels from my surely swollen lips, across my chest and down to where my fingers are gripping his shorts.

He flicks his gaze back to mine before asking, "Is that where you want your hands?"

I blush and shake my head.

"Use your words, Grace. I need to hear you," he says, running his fingers across my tight nipples and succeeding in pulling a gasp from me.

"I want—more. I want to undress you," I pant.

"All in good time...and we have so much time," he says, reaching behind me and picking my hips off the counter. He settles me across his hips, allowing me to feel what's beneath the waistband of those shorts. Our bare chests are crushed together, causing my breaths to be shallow and I fear once again that I might pass out.

With every shift of his hips as he walks me across the apartment, I'm having to remind myself that this is just practice. That as real as this feels, it's not.

It takes everything in my power to bring my mind back to the reality of the situation. By the time we make it to the living room, I've resolved to end this session for today.

Weston drops me onto the couch and I look up to meet his light brown eyes, glimmering and absolutely devouring what he can see of me. The small linen skirt I have on isn't doing much to cover the rest of me, hiked up around my hips like it is. As much as I hate myself for what I'm about to do, I know it'll be worse if I let this continue. I won't be able to forgive myself if I let this keep going. I can't stop the feelings flooding into my brain and my heart. This needs to stop now. Before one of us gets hurt.

"Hey," I start, drawing Weston's attention to my face, "I think that's enough practice for today, yeah?"

Weston's face scrunches in confusion before smoothing back out and he pastes a fake smile on. "Oh, sure. Practice—that's right. We can stop for now."

I get suddenly self-conscious, unsure why I'm just now realizing that my shirt is in the kitchen while I'm in here. I cross my arms to cover myself and shimmy my hips to scoot to the edge of the couch.

I give Wes a closed-lip smile and say, "Alright well I'm going to change into something comfy and then we can watch Netflix or something? Unless you have something else you're wanting to do?"

"No, that sounds fine," he answers, running a hand through the longer strands of chestnut hair on top of his head. He seems distracted, but not angry. I let it go and stand to head to my room. He doesn't move so I'm forced to brush up against him as I navigate the coffee table. The sparks that jump across my skin have me blushing again, remembering all too vividly how his skin just felt heating mine.

It takes no time at all to reach my room and I push the door closed behind me. I press my back against it and just breathe for a second. *I'm in shock,* I think. I feel numb, but I'm almost sure it's because I'm no longer feeling that fire race through my veins. I have never felt this way with anyone. And that scares me more than anything else. I know I'm the one that presented this idea of friends with benefits to Wes, but I feel like I could want more. That's something I'm way too scared to tell him, though. But this intense heat between us will ruin our friendship more than that admission, I'm sure. We still have a few months before the wedding. I'll just have to get used to this feeling and keep the rest of it to myself.

Chapter 18

Weston

It's officially the week of July 4th and I am more than excited for a boat day. Especially since Grace won't be able to escape me in close confines. She's been a little more distant since our last "practice session" and I'm not sure why. I can't decide if she's nervous about how she feels about me or if she's discovering she's not into me at all and this will be work for her.

Obviously, I'm hoping for the former. But other than watching our shows, she hasn't been very vocal about anything. I know that I should tell her how I feel about her, but I don't think it's time. I'm afraid I'll just scare her away.

Grace comes out of her room, looking as beautiful as ever. She has on a cute red bikini with a shimmery see-through top and my favorite jean shorts. She's completed the look with a red, white and blue bandanna rolled and tied in a bow on top of her head.

"What?" she asks, eyeing me suspiciously.

"You're just so damn cute," I reply, honestly.

She blushes but actually smiles and says thanks. I look back down to the cooler I'm packing for us when I hear her say, "You also look very cute. The blue looks really good on you." I glance down, seeing the sky blue of my trunks and realize that our outfits complement each other very well.

I stand up, slinging the backpack cooler onto my shoulders and see her still looking at me. She blushes so beautifully, I want to keep making that happen.

"Did you pack sunscreen? We all know what you look like with a sunburn," she says, laughing at her own joke.

"Yes, buddy. I packed sunscreen, drinks and snacks. Do you mind grabbing some towels from the closet?"

"Already done!" she says, pointing down at her beach bag.

"Well, you ready to get going?" I ask, grabbing my keys from the bowl on the island.

"Sure thing, buddy," she responds, throwing the nickname back at me.

I just smile and walk to the door.

➽➝

Once we're on the boat, Grace settles into the spot beside me on the bow. I have my arm laid over the back of the seat, but she doesn't shy away from my touch like she was a week ago. She goes as far as resting back against my side as we're cruising on our way to the island on the lake. Kimmy swears this is the place to go. Everyone anchors and swims the shallows. There are places to set up a waterfront spot to eat and hang out.

Pulling up, I realize Kimmy is right. There are boats, people and music everywhere. I reach over into our cooler and grab two drinks, staying seated while Kimmy and Bruce get the boat anchored. I pop the tops off, handing one to Grace.

"Cheers," I say, tapping my can to hers.

Grace gives me a sweet smile and pulls away from my side

to take a sip of her drink. I miss the contact immediately and let my hand drop from the back of the seat onto her thigh. She cuts her eyes from her drink down to my hand, but doesn't make a move to shove me off. I just smile at her and lean in to whisper, "I love how warm your skin gets in the sun. Almost as hot as it gets under my touch."

She shivers at that and I lick my lips, drawing her gaze to my mouth. I want so badly to kiss her right now, but that would probably be too much for her. Like I said, I'm playing the long game here and I'll just have to wait until she comes around to me.

I pat her thigh and stand, holding my hand out to help her up. We're in a no-wake zone so there aren't any waves, but I don't know how her sea legs are faring today.

"You remember the last time we were on a boat together, spending most of the ride chucking up breakfast?" she asks, drawing a laugh from me.

"Absolutely I do. I definitely thought we were just hung over from the night before, until everyone started in."

We both laugh, making our way to the back of the boat. The water is shallow enough that we can all just step off the back. Grace takes my drink and I step in, letting the water rush up to my waist. It feels amazing and it's so clear, you can see your feet in the sand.

"Keep hold of the drinks, I'll just help you in," I tell Grace, wanting to put my hands on her.

"Yes sir," she says, causing me to fake a scowl. She's such a brat.

Placing my hands on her hips, I swing her down into the water with me, nestling her against my body for a moment before setting her on her feet. She gives me another sweet smile as she hands me my drink.

"Thanks, that was much better than having to jump in," she says.

"You're ever so welcome. Anything for my buddy," I reply with a wink. Grace just rolls her eyes and wades off to join our friends in the circle they've created.

I reach back onto the platform of the boat to grab the pool noodles I brought so we can relax in the water.

"Oh, thanks," Grace says when I hand her one. "I forgot you brought these."

I just smile and turn towards the group. Kimmy invited the group from brunch and another group from the ICU is parked next to us. There's music blasting from our boat but it's not so loud that I can't hear the conversation. They're talking about a new supervisor that got hired from outside of the system. I can barely focus, my thoughts continuously wandering to Grace.

Like she can read my mind, Grace turns to me and says, "Want to explore the island?"

That's not *all* I want to do, but that will be a good start. "Sure, buddy. Let's wander a bit."

I watch in utter fascination as I relive a teenage fantasy. Grace walking out of the lake, water dripping from her hair, down her back and over her curves. Her name is apt in a time like this, she's all lean muscle and long, tanned legs.

I'm transfixed by the image to the point that she has to turn around to ask if I'm coming with her. And like a lost puppy, I follow. Running a bit to catch up, I splash water on both of us, causing her to laugh. I would do anything to hear that laugh all the time.

We finally make our way up onto the beach and the sand feels cold beneath my feet. There's not much of a walk to the grassy area and we slip on our flip flops as we step onto the trail. There's a covered trail with enough shadows to keep the area cool. And provide some privacy.

I'm hoping that Grace is using this as a way to ask me for another "practice session." I'm letting her lead this, considering I'm the one asking her to fake an entire relationship.

I pull out my phone, snapping a few pictures of Grace looking up into the trees. She's so beautiful and I want to keep these memories forever. She would probably think I'm a creep if she saw how many candid photos I have of her in my phone.

I discreetly tuck it back into my pocket and move to catch up with her. She's still looking around at the light filtering through the trees and I wonder if she's thinking about how she would draw this. She thinks I don't know that she's sketching again, but I've been finding her colored pencil shavings around the apartment in random places. I want to sneak a peek at her book, but I'm not going to go in there while she's out. I'll just wait until she's ready to tell or show me.

Grace told me one time that she used to love to draw, but she lost her passion for it in high school due to stress and other interests. I don't remember her drawing in college, either. She doodled on her notes during class, but nothing serious.

"What'cha doin' back there?" she asks, turning slightly to look at me.

I answer with a smirk and a quickening of my pace. We've gotten deep enough into the trees to shield us from any prying eyes and I'm determined to take advantage. "Just looking at you," I say, moving close enough to pull her into my arms.

She giggles, but lets me pull her back against me. "You up for another bit of practice? As my girlfriend, I'll be wanting to pull you in for a kiss at random times, touching you almost all the time," I say, using our position to run my fingertips over the outside of her arm.

"As your girlfriend, I'd be overjoyed at the prospect. As your *fake* girlfriend, it's a sacrifice I'm willing to make for a new dress," she replies, turning to throw me a wink. I laugh, but can't help the feelings of guilt swirling through me.

She's just trying to make me happy, but I'm trying to make her mine.

Chapter 19

Grace

I feel a rush of shame, knowing that Weston just thinks this is fake for me. It took me a while, but I've started to slowly realize that he's not joking when he says those sweet things. And he's not holding back when he kisses me, either.

All thoughts flee my head as he proves that yet again. With my back pressed against his chest, he slides his hand from my arm across my chest, up my neck and onto my cheek. He applies enough pressure to pull my mouth to his, immediately restarting that electric undercurrent. Weston snakes his other arm around my waist and pulls me back tighter against him. I gasp, allowing him full access and he takes advantage. Slipping his tongue past my lips, he sends lightning through my veins.

He removes his hand from my waist, leaving me bereft for a moment before he uses that hand to spin me to face him. Our heaving chests are pressed together as he pulls back to look down into my eyes.

"I really like kissing you," he says, so intense I'm near-quivering in his grasp.

I just nod my head, unable to speak.

He huffs out a hoarse laugh before saying, "Well buddy, we should probably get back before our friends miss us."

I just nod again, confused by the sudden change in direction. Usually our "sessions" last much longer. I think he can see the disappointment on my face, however, because he gives me a mischievous grin and a wink.

Exasperated by the way he just left me wanting so much more—but unable to express that thought aloud—I follow him back out from under the trees and down to the beach.

When we arrive back at the group, our friends are discussing plans for tonight. It sounds like everyone is going back to Kimmy's house for fireworks and more drinking. That might be just what I need. Some time with friends and with the ability to distance myself from Weston a bit. *Like that's what you really want,* I remind myself. If you won't be honest with yourself, who will?

Bruce is talking to some of Weston's friends about the setup of the firework show. "Oh dude, it's gonna be epic," Bruce says, more excited than I think I've ever seen him.

"When's the last time you watched a firework show?" Wes asks from behind me. With my eyes? It's been a while. I've been feeling them for a while now.

"A few years at least, I usually end up working on the 4th," I reply, turning to face him in the water.

"Really? I try to get off if I can—it's my family's favorite holiday. This is the first year in a while that I haven't been with at least some of them," Weston says, keeping his eyes trained off to the side. He really does love his sisters and his mom. That's one of his best features.

He's also one of the most emotionally mature men I've ever

met. I'm sure four older sisters will do that for you. Losing his dad a few years ago really changed his attitude. I remember going to the funeral with Lexa and Ansley. Brian had even commented that you could see Weston already weighed down, being the "man of the family" now that his dad was gone.

"Does your family usually do a show or go to one?" I ask, always wanting to learn more about him.

"It depends. If Tessa is around, she wants to perform the show for us. Otherwise, we drive over to the neighboring street where they shoot them off in a big open field." He gets a sweet smile on his face, obviously reminiscing.

"So Tessa is the fire bug in the family?" I ask, laughing.

He responds in the affirmative, nodding emphatically.

Conversation reverts back to tonight, and what games we'll be playing. Bruce suggests flip cup, which gets vetoed by most everyone. The consensus seems to be that we are too old for such a game.

I suggest at least a round of Jenga, the drunken kind of course. "Oh hell yeah, that's my favorite!" Kimmy nearly shouts. *I'm glad that we have a designated driver for the trip back*, I think.

As soon as that thought crosses my mind, our DD Freddy yells across the distance between the boats, "Everyone ready to head back? It's time for drinking games and shooting off some fireworks."

A chorus of cheers sounds as the two boats crank and ready to raise anchor. We all huddle back onto the boats, the steps slippery from so many wet bodies climbing the ladder.

I make it to the top rung before my foot decides to disobey my brain and misses the last step onto the deck. My shriek of fear gets caught in my throat, as I see the deck rushing up at my face. Dramatically, my life flashes before my eyes. Alcohol will bring all your worst tendencies to the forefront, of course—one of mine being a flair for drama.

The air rushes from my lungs as a strong arm bands across my chest. I'm pulled backwards into the water and straight up against Weston's hard body.

"Whoa there, buddy," he breathes against my ear. "You okay?"

"Yeah, thanks. That was close."

"We'd hate to bust that gorgeous mug of yours," he says, laughing.

I roll my eyes, but still smile. I'm so thankful he continues to be here.

It takes me a minute to realize that I'm still being cradled to Weston's chest, my legs floating under me in the water. I try to turn in his grip, but his arm is holding me close enough that I can't spin. "Are you going to let me go sometime today?" I ask.

"I would prefer not to, but if you're that ready to get away from me..."

I stop squirming immediately, relaxing into his hold. Of course I'm not ready for him to let me go. Unfortunately, he doesn't listen to my brainwaves and decides to release me from his arms. I nod, already missing the warmth. I wade back to the ladder, making it all the way up to the deck this time.

With no further incidents, we make it to land and to the cars. We pile in and head to Kimmy's house.

The next thing I know, Weston and I are seated on the couch, knee to knee and hip to hip. I pull my block from the tower, reading the scribbled words telling me to pick a partner and take a shot aloud. I laugh hysterically, leaning my shoulder into Weston's chest and looking up into his too handsome face.

"I choose you," I say, my words coming out with more gravity than I intended. I can tell Wes can feel the emotion behind the words by the way his gaze heats. I rip my eyes from roaming over his lips and force some lightness into the situation. "Shots, buddy?"

"Bottoms up, buttercup," he responds, licking his lips and drawing my gaze right back.

We each down our shot, gasping from the burn of the cinnamon. Bruce smacks Weston on the back a few times, trying to help him clear his throat. A round of laughter and insults circles the table and the heaviness of the moment finally dissipates.

After way more than one round of drunken Jenga, it's finally time for fireworks. We stumble our way outside, ready to see something amazing. The fact that Kimmy has a bed already made up for me to sleep in and sheets for Weston's night on the couch makes me so happy and grateful.

It makes it so much easier to let go and have fun.

In the vein of letting go, I've been flirting with Weston way more than I should. There's been a lot of touching. Not always innocent touching. His hands have been on my hips and my butt for the majority of our time at Kimmy's. He's "helping me to my seat" or "celebrating a Jenga win."

In reality, he's just been drinking all day and gotten handsy. But I don't mind, so I'm not going to tell him to stop.

In the dark, we all walk to the edge of Kim's big backyard where she has chairs and blankets set up. Wes uses the cover of night to lead me to a blanket and settles me in between his legs. He pulls me back against his chest so that I'm resting fully on him. He then leans back onto his hands and pulls his knees up to cradle me. I feel so secure and safe in this moment,

I don't think I could move even if I wanted to.

The fireworks begin, but it's hard to focus on the show in front of me with so much electricity running between me and the man behind me.

Chapter 20

Weston

You would think with the amount of times we've moved in the last year, we'd be better at it. For whatever reason, it still takes us several tries to get everything crammed in the car. We don't even have furniture.

"If you didn't have enough clothes to fill three closets, this might go a little smoother," I say, resting my hands on my hips. I finally shoved Grace's last suitcase into the cargo area of my SUV and have enough room in the backseat to fit our snack and drink cooler.

"Well, maybe if you didn't have to travel with a game system..." Grace says, but cuts off when she sees my face.

"If I didn't have my console, I'd be constantly pestering you to hang out. I'm sure you wouldn't want that, right?"

Her face colors beautifully across her cheekbones, drawing my gaze down and to her mouth.

And like the little heathen she is, Grace licks her lips, causing a wicked grin to pull at mine.

I quickly pull her to me and take her mouth, relishing in her taste. Even though she'd never admit it, I know she loves this. She may never let herself fall, but she'll continue to let me make her feel good. And I'll take what I can get for now.

I pull away, not wanting to get too carried away in the street. Grace smiles so sweetly at me, it's easy to forget we're not actually together. Yet.

"Are we all packed? Just the cooler is left?" she asks, pulling me from my thoughts.

"Yep! All packed and ready to go. I'll head back up and grab it if you want to get the car started so it can be cooling off," I respond.

"I call shotgun first!" she shouts, laughing maniacally.

I just shake my head, well aware that she is a passenger princess through and through.

As I walk back down the stairs, cooler in hand, I can't help but think this is a bittersweet moment. On one hand, I'm excited to move on to a new place with new experiences. But, this apartment will always be the first place I ever kissed Grace. And that feels monumental. I took pictures on my phone of the kitchen counter and the front door, wanting to always remember what those places mean to me. Maybe I'll have the entire layout of our next apartment photographed. Wouldn't that be something?

I sling the bag into the small space in the backseat, ready to finally get on the road. It's an eight and a half hour drive without stops. And we will definitely be stopping. Grace and I both prefer to find a good place for a sit-down meal halfway through the trip so we have a chance to get out of the car. It's even better if we can find a place with outdoor seating. Maybe we can find a good spot to grab some grub near Crater Lake National Park. That's about halfway and we can cross it off of the road trip list we started at the beginning of this whole thing.

I climb into the driver's seat and smile to myself, seeing that Grace is already settled in with her blanket in easy reach, her drink nestled in the cup holder and her sketchbook and pencils in her lap. I've never seen her draw in the car. Maybe I'll actually be able to catch a glimpse of what she's been working on.

When I've asked her recently if she has anything to show me yet, she always says no. The way she blushes, I'm assuming she's just not ready for anyone to see. I know her late grandmother always encouraged her artistic side, but maybe no one ever really praised her abilities.

But the way her hands make my skin feel, there's no telling what she can produce with a pencil and paper.

I turn on the radio, knowing that Grace prefers a car nap for the first hour of trips. Then we stop for coffee and she's ready to face the day. I wish these things didn't make her even more attractive to me, but there's no hope at this point.

Getting to watch Grace sleep in the car is one of my guilty pleasures. She always curls up in the seat and I have never seen anyone fall asleep as quickly as she does. I don't know if it's because she works the night shift or if it's a skill she's always possessed, but I'm jealous.

She's already softly snoring by the time we make it to the highway. I turn the volume down, not wanting to wake her. As the miles flash by, I'm taken back to last week and the night of the Fourth of July. I pulled Grace onto that blanket with me and she nestled into a comfortable position almost immediately. We sat like that for what felt like hours. Grace watched the sky light up with fireworks and I watched her light up with joy. I'm not sure that my eyes moved from her profile that night.

When it was time to go inside, I walked her to the door of the room she was sleeping in and as much as I wanted to go in with her, I didn't. I gave her a lingering kiss at the threshold and told her goodnight, then slept on a lumpy couch. I was not going to share a bed with Grace for the first time when she'd been drinking all day. While I still trust her to make those kinds of decisions for herself, I'm not going to give her the opportunity to soberly regret a drunken decision.

We have so much time, I'm not going to let her waste a minute of it by regretting her actions.

Even if that means I have to wait.

Grace stirs in the passenger seat and I glance at the clock on the dashboard. It's been almost exactly an hour since she fell asleep. I begin looking at the exit signs that we pass, searching for a Starbucks or any other coffee shop that won't pull us too far off of the road. Just as I spot a sign for coffee, Grace begins mumbling about how she'll need some caffeine soon if I expect her to live.

God, she's dramatic—but I love it.

We exit the highway and I'm already in the drive thru line when she finally cracks an eye open. "What do you want to drink?" I ask, nudging her shoulder with my elbow.

She pops up so quickly in her seat, I'm surprised she doesn't pass out. "Ooh, this is a new place. Pull up by the sign so I can read their menu," she orders.

"Yes, your majesty," I reply, doing as she asks—as always. Although, I'm not sure why she needs to see a menu, I know she's going to want a—

"Large vanilla and caramel iced latte," she says, still leaning halfway over me to see out of the window. This is what she always orders, no matter where we go. But I'm not going to be the one who points out her predictability.

"Two full pumps of each, right?" I ask, already knowing the answer. In reply, Grace just smiles at me. I shake my head but pull up to the speaker and place our order.

Once the caffeine is secured, we get back on the highway. Three good sips into her drink, Grace comes fully awake. She begins talking about all of the weird things she saw in the ICU her last shift in Nevada, how much she's going to miss the friends we made there, and how excited she is to see what Oregon has to offer.

Grace is very easy to travel with. Although I give her a hard time about not wanting to drive, I know she would if I asked her to. But I like to drive, and as long as I have entertainment, I can do it for a long time. Grace is amazing at finding something to keep my interest—whether it's playing the alphabet game, the license plate game, belting out whatever is on the radio, or just being a comforting presence in the passenger seat, there's no one else I'd rather have on these drives.

Chapter 21

When we're halfway through our trip, I turn fully in my seat to look at Weston.

"Yes, I've already scoped out a lunch spot. You okay with somewhere near Crater Lake so we can mark another park off of our list while we're at it?" he asks, somehow knowing I was going to be asking about lunch plans.

"Any chance the place has outdoor seating? I'm feeling cooped up."

"It does, and I reserved an outdoor table," he replies, giving me a smug grin.

I huff out a sigh—he's always ahead of the game. "Keep your eyes on the road, buddy. Before you kill us both."

In response, Wes breaks into a full smile, showing off his perfect teeth and his little half-dimple in his left cheek. *Whoa, when did I start noticing that?*

As if echoing my own thoughts, Wes points at the book beside my leg and says, "I noticed you brought your sketchbook along. Planning on drawing a little of the landscape while we're out and about?"

"I don't really do nature," I say, shrugging my shoulders.

"Well, what do you like to draw? You've never let me see any of your work," he says, glancing at the book again.

"Maybe someday. I'm just...not ready yet." I can feel my face heating with a blush. There's no way he's seeing this sketchbook right now. Every page with a smudge of graphite on it depicts some part of him. From his eyes to his mouth to the corded muscles in his biceps—I think there's even a sketch of just his fingers in here. I jerk the book from the seat to my chest in a protective gesture, knowing there's no way he'd ever try to snatch it from me. If he wanted to see what was in it, he could have peeked any of the times I left it out last week. I didn't notice that I had not carried it to my room with me until I wandered out to the living room and saw it on the coffee table. I guess I'm just begging him to catch me in the act. But of course, Weston is way too good of a human to dig into my personal stuff like that. Ugh, I hate how much I love him for that. *As a friend of course*, I hastily remind myself.

"But, um, I guess you could say I try to capture moments? Or rather the way people look in them," I finally answer. "It's hard to explain."

"So...candid portraits?" Wes questions, turning to look at me again.

"Somewhat. It's not always their faces though. Sometimes it's the way a hand looks when it's gripping an object so hard the veins stand out or the way hair looks as it blows in the wind or the ways pupils dilate when the person is attracted to someone...," I trail off as I meet Weston's eyes.

"Would I happen to be in that book of yours?" he asks, smirking.

"No, I have plenty of other muses. Thank you very much," I

respond, rolling my eyes. I berate myself for even mentioning that last part about the pupils, knowing full well Weston would catch onto me.

Just to tempt fate, I pull my book from my chest and flip to an empty page. I grab a pencil and start sketching the way one of Wes's hands is loosely gripping the wheel and the other is lounging on the gear shift. I've already memorized the shape of these particular hands, but I love capturing the way the tendons flex and veins pop with movement.

I see Weston turn his head every so often, glancing at my work. I try to stay focused, not wanting to miss any beautiful details.

My pencil flies across the paper, shading and shadowing with just the gray. When I'm satisfied, I start in with the colors—blending, deepening and shaping—until I feel that I've caught the essence of what it feels like to have those hands stretched across the steering wheel like it's your own skin.

I feel a smirk pull across my lips as I finish, knowing that he can see what I just drew. But when I look at him, he's still watching the road. Weston gives no indication that he's seen anything strange.

"Wanna see?" I ask, nervous that he's put off by the fact that I just sketched part of him.

"Do you want to show me?" he replies, teasing me.

I just smile, nod and flip my book around.

"Are those...my hands?" Weston asks, examining my sketch a little too thoroughly while driving.

"If I say yes, will you look back at the road?"

He just laughs and turns his head back to the front. I see a small smile still lingering before he quips, "I thought I wasn't your muse."

"Well, there's no one else in the car smarty pants. So it has to be you. I can always call up memories of past lovers and start sketching those for you," I snark.

"No, that won't be necessary little Picasso."

"Little?"

"Average height?"

"Just because you're a giant doesn't make me little or even average height. I've always been the tallest of my girl friends," I say, gesturing my hand around at nothing in particular.

Weston just laughs again, apparently intent on aggravating me on this trip. My mind flashes back to the way-too-short kiss outside of the car before we got started this morning. I was in no way prepared for it to begin and definitely not ready for it to end.

"Are you trying to get me riled up?" I ask, cutting my eyes at him.

"Maybe. I do like you all hot and bothered," he replies coolly, throwing me a wink.

I open my mouth to discuss this further, but I'm interrupted by the sudden turn of the vehicle off of the road onto gravel. The bumping of the SUV jars me and causes me to drop my book and pencils onto the floorboards.

"Shit," I curse, scrambling to keep the pencils from rolling away from me. I really don't want to be searching for these dang things under the seat instead of eating. The gravel under the tires is causing the pencils to bounce around like popcorn in the microwave. I huff and fling myself back into the seat, giving up. I'd rather not bang my head on the dashboard and get a concussion.

I see Weston's shoulders moving up and down, and incorrectly assume it's from the roughness of the road. That mistake it corrected when I hear a rough chuckle slip past his lips. I whip my head towards the man, fuming at the audacity.

"Excuse me, do you find something funny?" I demand, crossing my arms and giving a full head tilt. I want him to know just how much trouble he's in.

"You're just so damn cute when you're frustrated. I'm sorry buddy, I didn't mean to laugh at you," he says, softening me like butter. Weston reaches his hand across the console and pries my arms apart, taking my hand and giving it a quick squeeze.

I can't help but grin, knowing that he's being genuine. "Okay, well whatever." There's no venom behind my words and I realize I sound like a sullen teenager. I decide there's no reason to hold back my next question, "Are we there yet? I'm starving."

Weston's snicker turns into a full laugh, gifting his perfect smile to the world. I'm transfixed for a moment, but gather myself enough to look away before he catches me staring. I know what's going to be taking up the next page in the sketchbook. If I ever find all of my pencils, that is.

We're pulling up to the restaurant by the time I realize Weston never let go of my hand.

Chapter 22

Weston

There's no denying how I'm feeling about Grace anymore. I should never have agreed to this "friends with benefits" plan. But, it's the only way I'm going to get to touch her and be with her for now. I know she's still not looking for anything serious, though that's not going to stop me from continuing to show her how good I would be for her.

She's the first thing I think about when I wake up and the last thing on my mind each night. Getting to spend these uninterrupted hours with her on this move to Oregon has been great. We just made it to the new place with plenty of daylight left to get our stuff upstairs.

I don't know how she can deny the chemistry between us when I feel a jolt of electric energy every time our arms brush when we pass. Maybe she's just chalking it up to attraction.

Either way, I feel like my hair should be standing on end from all of the static humming through my veins.

I love that there are so many furnished apartments out there for rent for nomads like us, because as soon as we get done hauling our crap upstairs, I collapse onto the couch.

"Pizza?" I ask, pulling out my phone.

"Pizza," Grace agrees, dropping down onto the couch beside me. We scroll the menu of a place on our block and decide on something with a large amount of protein.

"Website says 30 minutes, want to queue up something to watch and we can start a movie when I get back with the food?" I ask, reaching over to place a hand on her leg. She no longer jerks at my touch and she even seems not to notice sometimes. All steps in the right direction. Of course, she thinks she's getting used to me touching her so that we can perform for my family. I can't wait to disabuse her of that notion. Another time, though. For now, I watch as she instantly toggles to the horror section. I chuckle as I see her pick a new one that I've heard is nightmare-inducing. That only means lots of cuddling on the couch so she can stay safe from the imaginary monsters.

We both play on our phones for a bit, relaxing before I walk over to grab the pizza. It's moments like this that I know we're perfect for each other. Grace has dropped her free hand onto my arm that's still resting on her leg. We're sitting in companionable silence and it just feels right.

An alert sounds on my phone, letting me know that the pizza will be ready in 5 minutes. I pat Grace's leg, and go to stand. I'm not sure she realizes what she does, but she grazes her hand down my arm and squeezes my fingers before letting go. It was a sweet little goodbye and not one that I've seen friends do very often. Maybe I'm underestimating her feelings for me.

I shake my head, telling her I'll be right back. I use the walk to clear my thoughts, trying to contain my excitement at the prospect that Grace might be starting to come around. I need to take this slow and rushing back up there and demanding her to tell me how she feels is just the opposite. So I vow to myself to continue my long game.

I get back with the pizza to see that Grace is snuggled up on the couch with her blanket and her phone. She looks so beautiful, hair in a messy bun on her head and no makeup on. I wish she would believe me if I told her. But I know that she would just smile and shake her head, unwilling to trust that I'm being serious.

I pull two plates from our new cupboard and grab two slices for each of us. "What do you want to drink?" I ask Grace, pulling a soda from the cooler for myself.

"What? Oh, I already have something," Grace rushes out, hurrying to sit up on the couch.

"You don't have to move on my account, there's still plenty of room," I say, bringing the plates and my drink to the living room.

She blushes and as much as I wish I could, I can't read this situation at all. Rather than continue to try to puzzle it out, I ask, "Why are you acting weird, buddy?"

Grace whips her head towards me, scowling under the intensified blush. "I'm not acting weird. You're acting weird. I'm just hungry."

Okay...whatever. I reach down to grab the remote, more than ready to start the movie and end this awkwardness, but Grace gets there first, causing me to wrap my hand around hers.

She jumps—actually jumps—and scoots to the end of the sofa.

"Yep, not acting weird at all...," I say, turning on the movie and trying to ignore the situation at this point.

What was she doing on her phone when I got here? Is that

why she's acting so skittish? Maybe she was texting another guy or finally installed a dating app like she always talks about doing and doesn't want me to see.

It would be mighty inconvenient if she decided to really start dating now. We'd have to go to the wedding and act like we're together while she left a new partner at home for the night? Yeah that's not going to work.

I have half a mind to ask her, but I don't want her to think I'm accusing her of anything either. It's not like we *are* dating, I don't have a right to pry into her life like that.

Just as we get the movie going, I see the screen of her phone light up. Against my better judgment, I look down at the phone. There's a new message and it only takes me a second to read Lexa's name as the contact. I exhale a sigh of relief, not realizing that I even had that much anxiety pent up over the situation.

Grace snatches her phone off the table and swipes to open the message, carefully shielding the screen from me. What could she possibly be hiding in a text from Lexa? Her face colors again as she notices me looking at her.

"Watch the movie, weirdo," she snaps.

I just chuckle and turn my attention back to the screen. Just in time for the first jump scare. I startle and Grace laughs. I pivot my upper body to face her, my mouth still open in surprise.

"Are you even watching?" I demand, knowing that she would have screamed if she had been paying attention.

Grace ducks her head, shaking it slightly.

"Put your phone down, then," I snark.

"You're not watching the movie, either," she retorts, making a decent point.

I grab the remote and pause the film, "There. I'll rewind to the scary part so you can have nightmares, too."

"Oh, thanks buddy. You're just too sweet," she purrs.

I laugh, rewinding to the moment before the jump scare and pressing play. Since I've already watched the scene, I watch Grace instead. This is another reason I love watching these movies with her—her face shows everything.

The scene plays and Grace jumps, her mouth rounding in an "O." Her eyes widen at the shock and her hands clench together under her chin.

"You knew it was coming and you still got scared," I say, laughing.

"Oh shut up!" she says, slapping my arm.

I pull her to me using that hand and force her to my side, "Don't worry, I'll keep you safe from the scary monsters. I got you, buddy."

She settles into me easily, letting me continue to hold her hand. As the movie progresses into more scary events, I notice Grace gluing herself to my side. Her legs are thrown over my lap and she's underneath my arm. This is much more cuddling than I'm accustomed to during our movie nights, not that I'm complaining. Instead, I wrap my free around her leg and massage her calf gently, aware that she's hardly paying attention to me.

Or so I thought. With each press and release of my fingers, I can feel her body moving in a similar motion. She's responding to my touch in a way that makes me want to turn off this movie and take this party elsewhere.

As if sensing my thoughts, Grace's focus leaves the TV and her hands fly to my chest.

She grabs my shirt, pulling me to her and presses her lips to mine. All other thoughts flee my brain as she kisses me.

I move my hand from her shoulders down her back and to her hip. I use my other hand to move her closest leg from my lap. In one motion, I pull her leg over me and use her momentum to have her straddling me. She gasps in surprise but doesn't stop the movement.

I shift my hand up to her hair, pulling the bun down to let her waves flow over her shoulders. Using my grip at the base of her skull, I lower her mouth back down to mine. Once our lips are touching again, she sighs and starts to move on top of me. Her hips circle in time with her tongue in my mouth, pulling a groan from my throat.

Grace slides her hands from my face, down my chest and to my stomach before thrusting them up under my shirt. I know what she wants so I pull away just enough to let her rip my tee off. I immediately find her lips again, letting her feel her way around my body. Her hands still at the top of my sweatpants, her fingers dipping slightly into the waistband. She retreats from me, eyes moving hungrily down my body and chest heaving as her breath comes out in pants. When she looks back up, I'm licking my swollen lips.

Something changes in her eyes as she tracks the movement of my tongue. Her already dark eyes morph to near-black and her mouth drops open. With no warning, she's back on me, kissing me hard enough to bruise. And I am loving every minute of it.

Chapter 23

Grace

Suddenly I'm ravenous for this gorgeous hunk of man underneath me. Wes took me by surprise pulling me over onto his lap, but damn if I'm not enjoying it.

As soon as I took his shirt off, I wanted to strip him of his sweats too. But that can wait. I'm having a hard time moving away from his mouth. He's perfectly edible and I know he was tempting me with that little tongue move. I bit hard on the bait, but he's not getting off of my hook anytime soon.

With a few well-timed nips and some hard-to-control breathy moans, Wes is coming apart at the seams.

I try to withdraw from his lap, intending to lead him to another location, namely one of our beds. But he seems to have other plans. His grip on my hair tightens as he twines it through his fingers and uses it as a leash. His other hand clenches onto my waist, not allowing any wiggle room and denying me any of the delicious friction I was working hard to establish.

"Where do you think you're going?" Wes growls, pulling me

impossibly closer.

I squeal and blush, never having seen this side of Weston before. Hot damn.

Unable to contain it, I let a whimper escape. Weston's lips curl for an instant before he's devouring me again. He wastes no time in removing the big t-shirt I had thrown on. I probably should have been wearing a bra, because now I'm completely bare to him aside from my underwear.

Weston growls again, this time in appreciation as his hands feel their way around my nakedness.

I mewl and try to move to initiate some sort of friction again. Moving my hips is next to impossible with Weston's grip on me, but he finally relents. I take full advantage, circling my hips on his lap and pulling a groan from deep in his chest.

There's nothing stopping us from taking this further tonight, besides our own issues. I don't know if Weston is wanting to go there with me. Fake dating doesn't really have to involve the whole package. We only have to kiss and hold hands convincingly, but we're far beyond that at this point.

Weston's hands roam over my back, following my spine and causing a shiver to run through me. I feel him smile against my lips and I know he can feel what he's doing to me.

I have never been so thankful for and simultaneously extremely aggravated because of a pair of sweatpants in my life. But Weston's are both in my way and saving us from potential disaster right now. It's hard to tell what Weston is wanting. He stopped me from moving us but he has such a firm grip on my ass right now that he's basically controlling my movements on top of him. And he's not slowing down.

I haven't made out with someone this long since high school. Usually partners attempt to skip all of this fun stuff and move on quickly to other things. But damn, the way Weston kisses should be illegal. It feels like he's sucking my soul from my body while soothing every burn and ache in its place. And of course the electricity is otherworldly.

One of his hands moves excruciatingly slow from my ass, up my side, before he flicks the hardened peak of my nipple. I gasp, allowing him further access to my mouth. As he charts a new course with his tongue, his hand comes to rest at the base of my skull, once again wrapping my hair around like a restraint.

He uses his grip to pull my head back and moves his mouth down my chin, then my neck. He finds that sensitive spot between my shoulder and collarbone and begins to drive me wild. I don't notice my back arching until I've forced my breasts to his face. He greedily takes a nipple in between his lips and then his teeth. I can't hold back the animalistic groan that rips free from my throat.

Weston releases me from his mouth and sits back, a satisfied grin stretching his sinful lips.

"You okay there, buddy?" he asks, not taking his hand from my hip or my hair.

I realize I'm panting, but I can't slow my breathing, still riding a thin line. When I don't respond verbally, Weston just smiles and leans in to give me another quick kiss on the lips.

"So, you were just wearing the shirt and panties, huh? Bold choice." He smirks, knowing that I'm not in the head space for a conversation right now.

"Well, I wasn't expecting you to pull me onto your lap and have your way with me," I quip lamely, not able to think of a more clever response.

"Mmm, you think that's all I wanted to do to you?" His eyes

glint with that hidden ferocity.

I blush furiously and remain silent. I reach for my shirt, needing less skin to skin contact to be able to think clearly.

Weston's hand circles my wrist, stopping me from slipping into my tee.

"Don't you want to finish the movie?" he asks quietly, eyes hooded and pupils blown.

I struggle for words for a moment before I settle on, "Well yes, but clothed."

"Is a t-shirt what you consider to be clothed?" he asks, tilting his head slightly, eyes never leaving mine.

"It's not naked. And that's what I am without it. So if you'd be so kind, I'd like to replace it." A blush steals across my face again, knowing that I'm basically asking for permission while also hoping he won't give it.

His eyes roam over my face thoroughly before slipping down for one last look before releasing my hand and letting me pull my shirt back on.

I exhale slowly and pull my leg over his lap to settle back in beside him. He only watches me with a look of total fascination on his face, a small smile on his lips.

"Do you want me to rewind to the last part you saw...?" he says, quirking an eyebrow at me.

"Oh shut up. I haven't been watching it for an hour and you know that. Asshole."

Weston laughs so loudly it makes me smile. I love that laugh. My smile falters slightly as I begin to realize that I'm screwed. I went and fell in love with my best friend.

Chapter 24

Weston

After a full week of settling in, we've started at our new hospital. It seems pretty nice so far. There is one huge drawback, however. Grace and I are basically on opposite schedules.

Aside from our movie night last week, I've barely seen her. Grace is asleep on my off days and I've been getting home late on her off nights. I still try my hardest to remind her that I'm thinking of her. I've been sending her texts throughout the nights she's at work and I'm at home, making sure there's coffee stocked and ready for her to just start when she wakes up and ensuring that I'm quiet while she's sleeping. It doesn't feel like enough, though. I need more time with her. If nothing else, to remind her that she's starting to like me.

Not that I think she might forget, I'm just nervous. More than ever now. We're a month away from the wedding and I'm worried she's just counting down the days. Every day we don't get to talk means another day I can't tell her how I'm really feeling.

She's at work tonight and I've texted her to have a good

night. She responded almost immediately that she got two settled patients so she's going to be mostly hanging out and helping others as necessary. That's a good change of pace, she usually gets the shit assignments as the travel nurse on the unit. Maybe these charge nurses are actually nice, for once.

Wanna play Sea Battle? I text, knowing she'll be down. It's a version of Battleship we can play through the phone and we play all the time. She has some supernatural ability to find my ships and wins almost every time, regardless how I arrange my battlefield.

Instead of a *yes*, I receive an invitation to the game and smile to myself. I strategically place my ships, hoping for at least a fighting chance. Within a few rounds, she's sank half of my fleet and I know it won't take much longer to finish me off.

Hold on a sec, Grace texts. She must have some patient care to do.

You know you don't have to text me to hold on when you're at work. I know you have things to do, I send back. I don't ever want to be a burden on her.

I flip through the channels on the TV, not in the mood for a video game tonight. I settle on *The Bachelor*, laughing when I realize that Grace has rubbed off on me in so many ways. I would never have willingly watched reality TV until she introduced me to it. Now it's something that soothes me, knowing that my mundane little life could never have that much drama.

I guess that's not necessarily true at this point in my life, having asked a woman that I like to pose as my girlfriend for my sister's wedding just to avoid the embarrassment that I would face from my family. Especially at the hands of my four older sisters. They love to rib me about my relationship status, or lack thereof recently. Tessa doesn't get the same treatment even though she's almost 40. She's just the cool aunt to my nieces and nephews. Autumn and Robert met at work 15 years ago and fell madly in love and Carmen met Lisa at a friend's wedding. They have the sweetest relationship and I'm happy for all of them but not when they won't leave me alone about *being alone.*

They love Grace, they've gotten to know her well over the last several years through our time in nursing school and now traveling together. But they have always maintained that we're perfect for each other. Even when Grace was with Brian.

I shake off these thoughts, trying to focus my attention back on these gorgeous and smart women vying for the attention of some douchey-looking DJ. *They could definitely do better*, I think.

It's an episode with a group date and all of the women are being required to try to DJ an event. It's funny how some of them are better at it than the lead guy, not that he'd ever admit to that.

That's something I've never understood. I want Grace to have the most confidence she could ever possess. Even if that means she eventually realizes she's way too good for me. It's better than her settling herself because of low self-esteem. And that's why I will continue to tell her how intelligent, clever, funny and beautiful she is—even when she doesn't believe me.

I know, but it's the polite thing to do, Grace texts back before playing me back in our game. And sinking another ship.

I sigh, knowing I'm a goner. In more than just this game.

Alright buddy, just finish me off. I can't take any more destruction. The fate of my fleet is in peril and the men are starting to falter, I text.

You are so weird, she responds—then hits my last two ships and send me a crown emoji.

Yes, you are the queen of the sea. We bow to your superior battle tactics, I type out, knowing it will make her laugh. And God, if that's not my favorite thing to do. If I was lucky enough to try to make Grace laugh for the rest of her life, I would gladly submit to the task.

Okay, well it's time for me to get some rest. We're not all night owls, I send, getting ready to head to bed.

I'm stopped in my tracks by the next text. *Goodnight buddy, dream of me ;).*

She must not know. It happens every damn night.

➤➤

My dreams kept me awake through most of the night. Each one was more vivid and stimulating than the last, causing me to wake up and stay that way for extended periods of time.

It's going to be long day of surgeries in the OR with little to no sleep. I stumble my way out of bed, hoping that I have a big enough thermos to bring a ton of coffee with me to work. I wander into the kitchen, but I'm stopped short by the book on the counter that I somehow missed last night. Grace's sketchbook is lying partially open, on a page with a nearly completed drawing. As I pass by, trying my hardest not to snoop, I realize that I'm seeing my hands. On closer inspection, I see my hands fisted in black hair. She even got the scar on my knuckle and the freckle on the outside of my hand. There's no mistaking it. I stand there dumbly, just staring at the drawing. Without opening the book, I'm able to tell this picture is very early on in her work, it's almost the first page. She got this book in St. Croix, so unless she's been tearing out pages, she was working on this after our interrupted moment that night on the island. Before we even talked about practicing for fake dating and before I had the chance to even kiss her.

I know she was sketching my hands on the ride here, she showed me. But this is different. This is…very different. I can't even put into words what I'm feeling right now. I need coffee before my brain can even begin processing what this means. Grace has *been* drawing me. Not just once. It makes me want to do something I swore I wouldn't. But I need to know if this was the only other time.

I shake my head, walking to the coffee maker and starting the brew function. I suck my lip between my teeth, chewing on it like it will give me the answers I'm searching for. The timer for the coffee dings and I pour a heaping cup, burning my mouth badly on the first sip. But the java immediately wakes up the rest of my brain cells and I'm warned off opening the book. Grace will show me her sketches when she's ready. And what does it really change if I'm scattered throughout it? We're together all the time, I'm probably just a familiar object to draw.

Chastising myself for even looking at the open page, I head back to my bedroom, ready to get started on the day. I need to get out of my head and focus on our cases. I have work to do.

Chapter 25

Grace

By all rights, I should be exhausted when I get home from my night shift in the ICU, but texting Weston to dream about me last night has left me giddy in an odd way. He didn't text me back but I can tell he read it. Was that too far?

I walk into the apartment, already dreading how quiet it will be. Wes works today. We're on such opposite schedules for the next several weeks and I hate it. The first thing I notice is the smell of coffee and I follow the lovely scent to its source. There's a note by the machine in Weston's handwriting.

Have a great day, gorgeous. I know you don't work tonight, so here's some freshly made coffee so you can relax with a hot cup and watch some gross reality TV.

I smile and then tear up slightly, aware that Weston knows me just a little too well.

The next thing I notice draws a gasp from my mouth. My sketchbook is on the counter, open to the first drawing I made of Weston back in St. Croix. I must have dropped it in my hurry to get ready last night. Maybe Wes didn't notice it. Surely he would have texted me to mess with me if he did.

Oh God, there's no way he didn't see it. It's on the way to the coffee maker. Thoughts war inside my head before I finally decide there's nothing I can do about it. Either he saw it or he didn't. If he saw it, there's still a chance that he didn't know it was him. I mean they're just hands. Hands that are very familiar and distinctive to me, but hands nonetheless.

I wrap both hands around my coffee cup, soaking the warmth into my suddenly cold body. I can really only hope that he didn't notice.

I wander to the laundry room in a daze, stripping off my scrubs and heading to the bathroom to shower. I barely feel the water on my skin or remember turning off the water and getting out. I shuffle back out to the living room, plucking the coffee cup from where I'd left it on the counter and silently settle on the couch. I turn on the TV, which is tuned to whatever Weston was watching last night. I finally break out of my head and laugh when I realize he was watching *The Bachelor.*

I'm awoken several hours later by the opening and closing of the apartment door. I startle awake, jerking up to a sitting position on the couch. I didn't even realize that I fell asleep out here. My eyes dart to my nearly dead phone to check the time. Weston has been getting home really late from work these days, I guess they have a lot of emergency surgeries here.

"Oh hey," Weston says, passing me on the way to the laundry room. He stops and turns to look at me fully.

"Hey," I reply, sleep roughening my voice. "You're home late."

"I know," he sighs, running a hand through his hair. My thoughts fly back to this morning, but he still hasn't said anything about the drawing. "We had several cases come in late in the day and they kept us even though they had called in the night crew."

"I'm sorry, buddy," I say, moving to stand up. I'm not sure why it's my first instinct. But right now, all I want to do it comfort him.

He accepts the hug I give him and pulls my face up to meet his. He kisses me gently before pulling back. "All better now," he says with a grin.

I blush and step back, thinking he probably is just ready to go to sleep. But he takes another step back to me, closing the distance between our bodies.

"I'm going to take a shower. Want to watch a show before I have to go to sleep? You pick," he says with a soft smile.

"Of course. I feel like I haven't seen you in weeks even though it's only been one."

"I know the feeling." His eyes roam across my face for a moment before he leans in to give me another soft kiss.

I watch as he strides into the laundry room to divest himself of his scrubs and then I'm greeted with the sight of Wes walking back across in nothing but his underwear. I blush—I can't wait for him to get back out here.

I don't have to wait long and before I know it, Weston is slouched on the couch next to me—shirtless. I cut a glance at him to find him smirking at me.

"What? If you don't have to wear pants, I don't have to wear a shirt," he says with a shrug.

"Fair enough," I say, turning my attention back to the screen like his bare body isn't heating me to the level of an inferno.

It takes only seconds before I'm sliding down the length of the couch, being pulled by strong hands. Those same hands run down the length of my body to my legs, which today are covered in sweat pants.

"Bummer," Weston breathes into my ear, making me shiver.

"I can take them off if you'd rather. It is getting warm in here, after all," I say, voice barely above a whisper.

"Let me help you with that," Wes replies. It's the only warning I get before my sweats are shoved down my legs and I'm drawn back into his lap. I'm breathing hard by the time I settle, looking deeply into the most delicious milk chocolate eyes.

"Thanks, I wasn't sure I would be able to get them off under the blanket," I say, quirking my eyebrow.

"Of course. Anything to help you out, buddy." And there's that wolfish grin, pulling his lips apart and showing me the teeth he wants to ravish me with.

I suck in a breath, but I'm not granted much of one before he's on me. Lips and teeth and tongue devouring me. I love the feel of his body under mine, I can't imagine anything better. Until he stands, holding me to him and begins to walk. The friction between our bodies is mind-blowing and I'm so caught up in the feeling that I don't bother to ask where we're going. I hear a door open and a moment later I'm in a soft set of sheets that aren't mine.

I look back up to Weston, who's towering over me with that unrestrained look in his eyes. Heat and desire are swirling through his massively blown pupils and I am lost in the current.

I should try to diffuse this situation, ask about his day or talk about the TV show we're supposed to be watching, but I can't. And I really don't want to. This moment is perfect and I'm not willing to spoil it.

All thoughts of leaving this room vanish as Weston leans

down, hands running up my bare thighs, over my hips and under my shirt. He uses one hand to sit me up and the other to pull my shirt off over my head. His breath stutters once before he's on top of me, using his momentum to propel me up the bed with him. I yelp, but any further cries are stifled by his lips on mine.

We fit together in a way that I've never felt before. It's like we were made for each other. I can't help but regret the time we spent not enjoying each other over the last year.

But then I may never have come to know the person that Weston is and that would be the real shame. The person I knew him as in nursing school has grown into the most thoughtful, loving and best friend I have ever had.

The way that his mouth is consuming me, however, is not anything like what I expected him to be. He's ferocious and I love it.

It's not until we're both fully naked that I finally realize maybe this is something we should talk about. But when I try to open my mouth to do just that, Weston reaches up and puts a finger to my lips.

"Shh, stop me if you want but I'm doing this because I want to, not because of some stupid lie." And that's all it takes to quiet my mind. Weston really does want me and want to be with me. There's no stopping this now.

⇒→

The light streaming through the blinds wakes me and it takes me a moment to get my bearings. I have blackout shades over my windows so there shouldn't be any sunlight.

And that's when I feel Weston move behind me, rolling over to snuggle into me.

I stiffen momentarily, but relax almost instantly into his

touch. He wraps a large arm over my body and pulls me back into him, making me giggle.

"Oh, you're awake?" he asks quietly.

I turn my head slightly and smile, "I am, aren't you supposed to be getting ready for work?" I have no idea what time it is, but I know he has to be there this morning.

"I still have about 15 minutes before I really have to get up. If I skip coffee, I can stay even longer," he laughs, nestling his chin into the crook of my neck.

"Or we could grab a shower and I'll make you some breakfast while you're getting ready?" I suggest, holding my breath—worried he'll reject me.

"A shower with you? That's the morning of my dreams. Let's go sleeping beauty."

He pulls me up from the bed, and picks me up to carry me into the bathroom. "I can walk you know. These legs don't just look good," I say, with fake consternation.

"Are you saying you don't like being carried around? It seemed to do it for you last night."

Immediately, a blush starts running across my cheeks. I smile, slightly embarrassed but fully grateful for the experience.

"So, do you want to talk about it?" I ask, not even sure that I do.

"What's there to talk about? We slept together and then *slept together*." He smiles at me and then turns to start the shower.

"Right, but where does that leave us?" I press.

"Wherever you want us to be. This can be a one-time thing, though I hope to hell it's not. Or we can just keep calling it our 'practice sessions' and seeing where it goes," he answers, shrugging a shoulder.

"You're leaving this decision fully in my hands, then?"

"Absolutely. I know what I want, I'm not going to force you one way or the other. At this point, I don't think anyone would doubt we were dating if we were to kiss or hold hands in front of them so that mission is accomplished. However much farther you want to take this, we can talk about it. You don't have to decide right now. We can shower, have breakfast and then I'll go to the hospital and you can think about it, okay?"

"That sounds...very reasonable. Okay, I'm in. Shower first though," I respond after a while, giving him my best reassuring smile.

All I can think is, *I'm in deep shit.*

Chapter 26

Weston

Mind-blowing. Life-altering. World-axis-flipping.

I cannot believe the night that I just spent with Grace. I had an indescribable night with the love of my life and then...then I told her that it could be the only time if that's what she wanted.

She can't want that. Not after last night.

I'm so beyond screwed and unable to even attempt to focus on my job today. We had breakfast and the morning went by way too fast. I wanted to stay and bask in our afterglow for much longer than half an hour. Instead, I had to get dressed and come to work and regret every choice I've made that led me to this point. That point being that I'm not at home with Grace right now.

I sigh and finally turn the water off. I can't scrub in for 40 minutes just because I want to use that time thinking about the woman I left at home.

I walk into the OR, fully sanitized and ready to face the case. Thankfully, it's just an appendectomy and my favorite surgeon is here. I've met three of them already but Dr. Shay is easily the best all-around. She's cool, smart, funny and very easy to get along with.

And she plays the best music. As I get to my spot, I start singing along to the Taylor Swift album she's playing. One of the countless amazing songs Miss Swift has put out.

I look around, seeing that everyone looks like they're ready to get started. Dr. Shay calls the time out and we discuss the patient, case and all the things that have to be talked about before we ever even touch the patient.

My mind can't drift where I want it to, I'm fully focused on the surgery and ensuring the best outcome for this patient. Mama didn't raise no fool.

We're about an hour into the surgery when I hear the music skip and Dr. Shay swear like a sailor.

"What do you need?" I ask from my station as the circulating nurse. I think ahead, trying to determine if she needs more sponges, another instrument or if she's just mad about the music skipping.

"A better WiFi connection, I guess," she says, shrugging.

I laugh, glad that the music is her only source of concern. I continue charting, counting the used sponges and making sure our vitals are staying in range. We're almost done at this rate.

The surgery is over in record time with probably the least amount of blood loss I've ever seen. I congratulate the team on our successful procedure and turn to leave the OR suite. Before I can make a complete exit, however, I hear my name being called.

"Hey, it's Wesley, right?" asks one of the scrub nurses, coming up to me to talk.

"Weston, but you can call me Wes," I reply, giving him a

smile.

"Oh, sorry man. I've just been seeing you around the last few weeks. You new here?"

"Yeah, I'm a travel nurse so I'm here for an eight week contract."

"Oh cool, I'm Ian," he says, sticking out a hand for me to shake.

"Hi Ian, you on the next case with O'Malley?"

"Indeed, I believe I'm circulating. You scrub?"

"Yep, ready for it, too. I'm very in my head today and need something to really pull me out," I say, oversharing a bit. *Oh well,* I think.

"Well, we have 45 minutes, do you want to run upstairs and grab a quick coffee? This next one is going to be a doozy and I need a boost."

"Sure, let me run to the restroom real fast and I'll meet you outside the OR doors." He gives me a thumbs up as I turn to go find the bathroom. *What a nerd,* I think. I like him already.

Once we make it to the coffee shop on the second floor, he starts in on the questions. The *where are you from* and *what do you do in your free time* set.

"I'm from Texas originally, but over the last year I've been all over the States. We've been traveling since last July. For fun, I hang out with my...travel partner and watch movies or play video games." I don't know why I stumbled so hard over what to call Grace. I want to call her my girlfriend, but to anyone but my family that just isn't true.

"You have another guy traveling with you?" he asks, taking a sip out of his cardboard cup.

"A woman, actually. Her name is Grace. We went to nursing school in Alabama together and then really reconnected at a friend's wedding last summer. She works in the ICU here on nights."

"Oh cool, are you two like together or...?"

I glance at him, trying to determine if he's just getting to know me or if he's way too interested in this line of questioning. He's just casually sipping his coffee, looking around the hall and then back to me when I don't answer immediately. So just trying to get to know me, then. "Um, no," is all I say. I don't feel like getting into this right now.

Ian has other thoughts apparently because he studies my face for a moment before saying, "Oh, but you want to be. That's too bad, man." He gives me a look like he's just seen a orphaned puppy at the pet store.

"Well, too be honest, that's why I'm in my head today. I'm not sure you want to hear about all of this, though." I shake my head, warning him that he really doesn't want to hear my sob story.

"I'm a sucker for unrequited love, so I'm always down for a story."

I shake my head again and against my better judgment, I launch into the story of Grace and I—leaving out the juiciest bits, of course.

By the time we're back in the OR, Ian knows everything I know about Grace and I. He left me at the threshold of the OR suite with, "We'll talk more after."

I didn't realize how good it would feel to talk to someone about all of this. But I feel lighter, and more assured already that I'm waiting for something important and life-changing. Grace is worth it.

Chapter 27

Grace

Spending a full day alone at the apartment after being with Weston last night has me pacing and going a bit stir crazy. Normally on my off days I would be watching a new show or reading, even sketching. But today, I feel like I can't sit down. I don't know what this means for us. I know when Weston said it was up to me, he wasn't lying. So I guess I need to do some soul-searching.

We have a month until the wedding, so it's not like we can just quit all of this cold turkey, even if I wanted to. We would look insanely awkward trying to rekindle a physical relationship the day of the rehearsal dinner. So we'll stay the course, for now. Does that mean more nights like last night? I wouldn't mind that. It's not like it's any different than us just living together. We're already spending all of our free time with just each other. That's not dating. It's just the way our friendship works.

There's no reason to change that label yet. That can wait until we're telling Weston's great-aunt that we're together, or whoever we happen to see at the wedding.

I still need to go get my dress and shoes, but I think I'm going to wait until next week for that. Weston and I have the whole of Wednesday off together, so I plan to make him go with me then. Can't have him backing out of his part of the deal, not that I would ever think he was *that kind of guy* anyway. I know him too well for that. But, it would be nice to get his real time input on what I pick out. It's his sister's wedding, after all.

I'm on my third cup of coffee by the time I realize that I haven't eaten breakfast and the shaking of my hands isn't going to stop on its own.

I laugh, startling at the sound of my own voice in the empty apartment. I really need to get a grip. I've been alone here before, but it's never felt this...lonely. I've quickly become addicted to the space that Weston takes up and the sound of his voice and laughter. The place feels somewhat barren when it's just me.

I decide to turn on some music while cooking, to ease some of the tension I'm feeling. I pick a playlist at random, just wanting the noise.

And of course it's all songs that would be the perfect backdrop for a romance novel. It's all about love and feelings. Which is not really what I need today. No music then.

The sizzling of the frying bacon is the only sound now. That and the enormous storm raging in my head. Why am I so averse to even thinking about a relationship with Weston? It's not like it would even change anything. We're basically dating now. It just feels like calling it that would ruin *everything*.

It's not like he's not willing to risk it, I remind myself. But am I? I don't want to lose him forever just because I'm not willing to commit to a different kind of future. And that's the ultimate issue. The reason that Brian and I broke up is still a problem for me. I don't want the whole white picket fence and 2.5 kids life. It's not for me. I want to travel, even if I end up buying a house somewhere, I don't want to feel stuck there. And that's how I would have felt with Brian. This past year of traveling with Weston has been amazing because there's no pressure to stay. The contracts we take are long enough that we make friends but not so long that I start feeling claustrophobic. And of course, Weston himself is so great. He's learned to recognize when I'm feeling stuck and we take little side trips when we're off work. This month has been rough due to our opposite scheduling, but September will be better. We work almost the same schedule until the wedding, so we'll be able to spend more time together.

Which, regardless of how I'm feeling about labels, I want to continue to spend time with Wes. I want to spend *all* of my time with him. It's a disconcerting realization. The same as when I look through my sketchbook and see that it's filled with him, my mind is just as singularly focused.

It feels silly to deprive myself of the possible intense happiness that I know I could find with Weston. But I can't hurt him, either. And I think, even though a lot of this has me stuck on not wanting to wreck our relationship we have built, I ultimately just don't want to hurt him. And letting this continue without any intention of having a real relationship afterward would certainly maim him.

Although, he did seem fine this morning. He offered to let last night be a one-time thing if that's what I want. Ugh, I just don't know what to do. I barely know how to interpret the feelings rushing through me, much less verbalize them for someone else.

If I was a good person, I would stop this or at least slow it down. I know if my emotions are getting wrapped up in this, Weston's just as involved. But I'm selfish. I know in the depths of my wretched heart that I'm going to let this play out, damn the consequences. I hope Weston survives this, because I don't know that I will.

Chapter 28

Weston

"We're going where?" I ask, pulling Grace into my chest as she attempts to roll out of the bed.

The fact that we haven't slept apart when we've both been home has me giddy. Even on days when she gets home and I'm not going in, she'll join me in bed and sleep the day in my room. I installed black out curtains over the weekend while she was at work, I didn't want her to sleep poorly in my room.

"To the dress shop," Grace says, voice muffled by my body. "You owe me a dress and shoes, remember? I think I've more than fulfilled my end of the bargain."

I laugh, but say, "Technically you haven't yet, we still have to convince my family that we're together."

I feel her squirming out of my hold, but she doesn't go far. She leans back to look me in the eye. "Yeah, we don't act like a couple at all. I'm sure they'll have a really hard time believing it."

But then she smiles her gorgeous, world-stopping smile up at me and my breath catches in my chest. I can't help but lean down and kiss her soft lips.

"Just five more minutes? I'm not ready to get up yet," I say, running my hands along her back and enjoying the arch of her body into mine.

"The stores don't open for another hour. We have all the time in the world," Grace replies with a gleam in her dark eyes.

≫→

We don't make it out of the apartment until lunch—my fault mostly. I couldn't keep my hands to myself. In the bed, or the shower, or the kitchen. But we're finally out and about. First stop is a little boutique several blocks from our place.

"Have you been here before?" I ask, reaching across the console of the car to hold Grace's hand.

"No, but I've been looking at their website and it looks like they have some really cute stuff. They didn't seem to have a huge selection of formal wear, but I figured with it being so close and on the way to the other places we might as well check it out. Shop small and all that."

"Sounds good to me," I say, bringing her hand up to my mouth. Planting a soft kiss on her palm, I glance over to see Grace staring at me with a mesmerized look on her face. Dark eyes wide open, mouth slightly parted and chest swollen with a deep inhale. "You okay, buddy?" I ask.

She shakes her head a bit, but mumbles that she's fine. I set her hand back down on her lap, fingers still intertwined with my own.

Once we pull up to the curb, I know I'm going to have to let go of her hand. But instead of just dropping it, I pull it back to my mouth and give it another quick kiss. Then I use my leverage to pull her over into my area and give her a not-so-quick kiss on the lips. I linger there, letting her steal my breath away.

She finally pulls back, much too soon for my liking. "If you keep this up, I'm not even going to want to go into the boutique. Then I'll have to show up to the wedding naked," she sighs, cutting her eyes to me.

"You say that like it isn't my dream," I reply, brandishing a wolfish grin.

"Oh stop it, we're going in," she says, still not moving her hand from my grip.

"You have to let go of me for either of us to get out of this car," I remind her gently.

"Oh. Oh right. Of course," Grace responds hastily, like she'd somehow forgotten we were just sitting here holding hands in the front seat of the SUV.

Grace takes a deep breath and in the span of a second, she's released my hand and flung her door open. I follow her lead, walking around the edge of the car to meet her on the sidewalk. I reach down to grab her hand again and surprise floods through me when she allows it.

"Well, let's get this over with," she mutters, looking ahead.

"Hey, you okay?" I stop her from walking forward, instead turning her to face me. I notice there's an odd set to her mouth, almost a grimace. Is she dreading this somehow? Maybe having the dress for the wedding just makes it more real for her that she's going to be lying to my family for me.

"Yeah, I'm just nervous I guess. I haven't tried on a nice dress in a while and I definitely haven't been working out. I just...want to look good on your arm," she finishes, avoiding my eyes as she stares at the ground.

I use my thumb and forefinger to tip her chin back so I can look at her face when I say, "Grace, you are the most beautiful woman I have ever known. Inside and out. Whatever you choose to wear, whether it's a silk gown or a flour sack, I'll still feel the same. It's an honor to be carrying you to this wedding. Now, get out of your head and let's go pick something that deserves to be on your gorgeous body, okay?" Her dark brown eyes widen with each word from my mouth. By the end of my little speech her eyes have grown glossy with tears. Before they can spill down her cheeks, I run the pads of my thumbs underneath them and bring her face to mine for a searing kiss.

I release her face and run my hands over her shoulders and grab each forearm. "And I don't ever want to hear that kind of negative self-talk again, okay?"

Grace smirks slightly, releases a long sigh and finally says, "Yes sir." An impish grin begins to form on her lips as she turns away from me.

I playfully swat her butt as she turns and reply, "Oh, don't be a brat darling." Grace just giggles and continues to strut into the boutique.

It hits me again just how hooked on this woman I am, but I'm too far in to care anymore. Instead, I just follow her into the store and prepare for a feast of the senses as she tries on dresses and shoes.

After searching through every rack in the store, Grace found at least six possibilities and they're all available in her size. I'm ushered onto a settee placed just outside of the dressing room entrance so that I can watch the fashion show. The owner of the boutique has been fawning over Grace since we arrived, knowing a good client when she sees one. A champagne glass in hand and an arm slung casually over the back of the couch, I feel very at ease here. I smile at the other customers as they file in and out of the racks. But my attention is captured by the silhouette of Grace in the dress she's just walked out in. Or strutted out in, rather. She's in a forest green satin number, gently hugging every curve of her body. She does a twirl for me as she reaches the end of her impromptu runway and the light plays off of her hair in such an enchanting way, I forget to breath for a moment. I chuckle darkly, knowing this dress would end up on my floor before we even made it to the event.

I draw Grace to me with a little come-hither gesture of my finger and whisper that exact sentiment into her ear. She gasps and flushes as she leans away from me, watching the devilish grin stretching my lips.

"So, this is a definite no," she says, laughing.

"Well that's up to you, buddy. It depends on how you want my sister's wedding night to end for you," I reply with a smirk. Her face flushes even deeper, knowing the other patrons most likely heard that.

As Grace straightens to stand, she grabs my champagne glass and takes a healthy swig before handing it back to me and returning to the dressing room.

"The back is even better than the front," I raise my voice slightly to make sure she hears me. I see a middle finger raised above the dressing room curtain and can't contain the peal of laughter it releases. God, this woman can really make me laugh. I don't remember a time I've been this happy this often.

We're down to the final dress, having been through a few navy blues, a black and a pretty orange number. None of them have been *the one.* But as Grace pulls the curtain to the side, revealing a long leg peeking through a slit in a gorgeous deep red gown, I know without a shadow of a doubt we're leaving the store with this one. She saunters towards me, the dress billowing at the hip from the cut of the bottom and her smile lights up the entire room. The attendant who handed us the drinks returns at this moment to offer an elated sigh. "This is the one!" she says, covering her mouth with her hands.

"You think so?" Grace asks, looking first at the woman and then to me.

"I love it, but what do you think?" I ask, knowing that smile stretching her face means she agrees.

"I feel beautiful," she says. She giggles for a second before thrusting her hands down her sides and exclaiming, "And it has pockets!"

"Of course it does. It's the perfect dress," I say with a laugh of my own. "Unless you're planning to wear it home, you can go get changed and I'll check out. Those are the shoes you're wanting?" I ask, gesturing to the nude shoes she's wearing.

"Yep!" she says, still gleaming.

"They complement the dress and your skin tone so well, love," the owner says, walking up to check the final look.

"Is it okay if I go ahead and check out while she's changing?" I ask, standing from the couch.

"That's perfect. Follow me right this way, doll," she answers, waving a hand towards the counter. "Just the dress and the shoes today, sir?"

I shake my head once before handing over an extra item. "Will those shoes look okay with this as well?" I ask.

The boutique owner smiles and nods, packing the extra item into the bag before ringing up our total. Grace joins me at the counter, not a hair out of place. The shop attendant had already brought her dress and shoes to the counter so Grace flutters up to me with a huge smile.

"Thank you for this. Not just the dress, but the day. This is the best shopping experience I have ever had. I can't believe I found the perfect dress at the first place we stopped." She reaches up on her tiptoes and gives me a soft kiss on the cheek.

"And we're here if you need us for anything else. The rehearsal dinner, date night, we have everything," the owner says, handing the bag over the counter.

Grace blushes and stutters out, "Oh we're not...we're just... thanks so much." She looks at me, hoping I'll help her out. Instead, I just grab her hand and kiss her palm again.

"Ready for some lunch, buddy?" I ask. And watch as her smile takes over her face again, eyes crinkling in the corners.

"Sure thing, buddy. Lead the way," she answers, letting me tow her out of the store. She turns to wave to the owner and the helpful attendant and then we're out on the sidewalk.

Chapter 29

Grace

I'm not sure when the term *buddy* transitioned into a term of endearment that I love to hear from Weston. The way he says it makes it sound like babe or sweetheart. But it's now my new favorite pet name.

I can't help the smile that's stuck on my face. The way his eyes were devouring me at the store set me on fire and it's going to be a long lunch.

I can't sit still, especially with the way he's still looking at me. I just want to get back to the apartment. But Weston is just sitting there, sipping his drink and smiling at me. *This asshole.*

"You gonna order something to eat?" I ask, leaning onto the table to rest my chin on my hands and giving him a sweet smile.

"I already know what I want," he says, a husky edge to his lowered voice.

"From the menu. I don't think what you're talking about is on here," I reply, huffing out a sigh. I roll my eyes for good measure, just to make sure he knows I'm irked.

Weston just laughs, knowing he's never going to make it on my bad side. He finally glances at the menu, ready to order something he can actually eat in public. I flush, the visual of me spread on the table before him popping unbidden into my mind.

"What's on your mind there, buddy? You got awfully red," Weston observes.

"Oh, um, nothing really," I splutter, unable to form a coherent thought as Weston's tongue works the straw against his lips in a very sinful manner.

"Mmm," he murmurs, still not taking his mouth away from the straw. He winks at me, knowing my thoughts have strayed into unsuitable territory to talk about in this restaurant.

I whip the menu up in front of my face, trying to hide my thoughts. Probably for nothing, but it doesn't hurt to try. I scan my eyes down the words, not really reading them. I'm sure I'll just go for my usual BLT, being a creature of habit. It's my current favorite meal.

Fingers curl under my menu, gripping and then flipping it from my hands. "I want to be able to see that gorgeous face," Weston says, taking the laminated plastic away and setting it on the table. "Plus, we both know you're getting a BLT and sweet potato fries."

I smile, loving how he knows me so well. It's so easy to be around Weston. My grin falters momentarily, remembering that this might be over after the wedding. He hasn't mentioned anything since saying he's wanting to settle in one spot. If he doesn't want to keep traveling, then I'm not sure how this is going to turn out. It feels like we're going in two different directions.

I'm not ready for this to be over. But we're not there yet. I make the vow once again to live in this moment and stop trying to plan for an uncertain future. In the spirit of this vow, I rip myself out of my own head and offer Weston another sweet smile. He responds by reaching across the table to grab my hand.

"I feel like you were gone there for a second. Where did you go?" he asks, squeezing my hand to reassure himself that I'm still there physically.

"Oh you know, just in my head. I'm back, though," I reply, giving another soft smile.

"Well, welcome back. I'm glad to have you here with me. Let's return to the important things—food," Weston says, laughing.

"Of course," I say, gesturing my hand to the menus in front of him. "Did you figure out what you're ordering?"

"Oh yeah, I knew before we even walked in here. Some of the people at work have been raving about this place's patty melt."

"You and your ability to make conversation about anything at work. When do you guys even have time to have these talks?" I ask, thinking about how most of my coworkers talk about everything but food at work.

"Well I hate to tell you this, but sometimes when we use certain instruments in the OR, it can smell like barbecue. And then we talk about food. It's a good thing our patients are asleep or I'm sure they would be horrified," he says, laughing.

"I'm a little horrified myself—not gonna lie." I shrug but force out a little laughter. I know he's talking about cauterizing flesh and it does have a certain smell. But not one that has ever given me any type of increased appetite.

"Good thing you're getting a BLT then!"

Chapter 30

Weston

After our enlightening lunch the other day, I've been trying to decide the best way to plan out a sitting session for Grace.

She expressed interest initially but hasn't mentioned it again. I'm not sure if she's just nervous about it or if she's decided she doesn't want to anymore. Either way, I want to show her that I'm more than willing. And I think the best way is to surprise her. That way she doesn't even have time to get in her head. We're coming up on a short stretch of off days together so I think I have at least the inkling of an idea.

I send her a quick text to determine if she already has plans. While I'm waiting for her response, I check into availability at some of the hotels in the area. We need a night or two that feel different than our norm. Somewhere we can be just two people out on a date. Maybe she'll realize that she's jumped that hurdle and we're already dating. And if not, at least she will see we can easily act like a couple in front of other people.

As I'm narrowing down choices for our stay, I receive a reply from Grace that she does not have plans and she would be delighted to hang out. Perfect. I go ahead and book a room. In the excitement of the moment, I decide to go ahead and pack a bag even though we won't be leaving until the day after tomorrow.

I make sure the present I bought from the boutique is packed and I run into Grace's room to grab her shoes from the other day, too. She'll never miss them. Luckily, she's not the most observant when it comes to her stuff. As evidenced by the fact that she had been leaving her sketchbook out and open.

While I'm bummed that Grace isn't home right now, it does make it easier to pack the things I'll need without her being able to see. I shoot her another text reminding her that I work tomorrow but I'll be home tomorrow night in time for dinner. She responds with a quick thumbs up and smiley face. I decide to hunt down her overnight bag and write her a quick note about what to pack. While I want most of this experience to be a surprise, she should at least have an idea of what to bring to wear during the day.

I write out my tentative itinerary on my phone, places I'm wanting to explore, making sure to just put vague items so she doesn't get too suspicious when she sees it.

I retreat to my room, knowing that I'll need to at least try to get some sleep. Work will be hard enough tomorrow morning, with this much anticipation for the following day. I'm going to be all in Ian's ear with this shit and I'm not even sorry.

As I lay staring at the ceiling, I replay scenes from the last several weeks in my mind. Things are so much easier between us than I could have ever imagined. Grace is perfect and I've never felt this content with anyone else. It's like the physical aspect of our relationship was just the natural continuation of our friendship.

I fall asleep with the sweetest smile seared into the back of my eyelids. And the darkest pair of eyes haunting my dreams.

≫→

I have to leave for work before Grace gets home, so I leave breakfast in the microwave and grab a bottle of red wine and a glass and place them on the counter for her. She texted me at one point last night while I was asleep that it was a bad night in the ICU, so I know she'll need to unwind a bit before she can fall asleep.

With the latest reality binge show cued up on the TV, I toss the remote back on the coffee table and give the apartment one last glance. Nothing too out of place that she'd notice what I have already packed in my bag. I smile to myself as I make my way out the door and down the stairs.

My good mood continues throughout the first two cases of our morning, bright enough that Ian starts looking at me funny. "You on something? If so, I'll take some, too," Ian says between our second and third surgery.

"No, just happy," I reply, shrugging. I know it's ridiculous, but it's true.

"So it's going well with the roommate then?"

"More than well. It's going great. We're having a little stay-cation in the area for a couple of nights starting tomorrow and I'm pumped. I have a few little surprises planned, too."

"Little?" Ian questions, pointedly glancing at the crotch of my scrub pants.

"Oh shut up," I say, shoving his shoulder with mine, keeping us both sterile as we scrub every germ particle from our hands at the sink.

And the rest of my workday passes like this—joking with Ian, rocking out on some cool surgeries with our doctors and trying to focus on anything but Grace. Not an easy task.

By the end of my shift, I'm tired and slightly sore from some of the stances I was in for hours today. But I'm ready to get home.

Ian calls my name across the hall and I turn to see him smiling and waving me down. "Hey bro, wanna grab a drink? A few of us are hitting the bar down the street since we have the day off tomorrow."

"Um," I start, nervous to say I really want to get home to my non-girlfriend. "Rain check? I'm pretty tired and I have some things I need to do around the apartment."

"I'll take that as Grace doesn't work tonight. Copy that. Don't worry about it," he says when he sees my horrified face. "Man, we've all been there. You're lucky you have someone to go home to, enjoy that." He claps his hand on my shoulder, still smiling without a trace of judgment.

"Okay, yeah. I'm serious about the rain check, though. I'd love to get together with everyone!" I'm already walking backwards as I say this, my body removing me from the building of its own accord.

The short drive home feels like an eternity, my leg bouncing enough to shake the vehicle. As I pull up to our building and start searching for a parking spot, I glance up at the window that belongs to our living room. I expect to see the flashing light of the TV and when I don't, I look down at the clock on the dash, wondering if I got home too early for her to be awake. But no, it's my normal arrival time. Weird, maybe she's holed up in her room.

I make my way up the stairs, unlock our door and push it open—immediately I'm assaulted by the delicious smell of Spanish cooking. And the sweet sound of Grace singing. She only sings when she's cooking. When I asked her about it one time, she seemed shocked. Apparently her mother sings in the kitchen and it somehow got passed down without Grace even realizing it.

I drop my bag by the door and kick out of my shoes. As I enter the kitchen, I see Grace. A lot of Grace. She's only wearing one of my t-shirts and though it's large on her, she has a lot of leg on display. I smile to myself and make my way to the distraction that's been on my mind all day.

"Hey beautiful," I say close to her ear, encircling her mid-section with my arms and pulling her to me softly. She smiles but doesn't stop her song, nor her stirring.

I rest my chin on her shoulder and soak in this intense sensation building in my chest. "It smells good," I say, instead of the "I love you" that threatens to slip out.

"Mmm, tastes good too. Here," Grace offers me the wooden spoon with a scoop of rice and shrimp on it.

"Girl, you know paella is my favorite. What's the occasion?" I ask, still keeping her wrapped in my arms.

"I'm just excited to have you home and to myself for the next few days," Grace says, leaning her head back against my shoulder, our cheeks resting side by side.

I hum my approval at that statement, unwilling to speak and ruin the beauty of this moment. This feels like so much more than coming home to my roommate. This just feels like coming home. The emotion starts building in my chest until I can't control it. I turn Grace away from the stove and take the wooden spoon from her hand, gently laying in on the spoon rest. I take her face in my hands and try to convey all of my unsaid feelings through a kiss. It'll never be enough, but it's almost enough for now. I pull back, smiling before I even open my eyes. When I do, I'm greeted with a flushed Grace, smiling beautifully at me. The ache in my chest only grows. But knowing that I can't say what I want to right now, I press a kiss to her forehead and reach for the spoon. I take up the stirring, seeing that the dish is almost done.

I can feel Grace's eyes on the side of my face but I don't turn to her yet. I'm afraid of what she'll see in mine.

Chapter 31

Grace

"So you never told me what you have planned for the next couple of days. You've only told me to pack and that we won't be here for the next two nights," I say, trying to get Weston to at least give me a hint.

We're sitting at the kitchen island, having just finished dinner. Not to brag, but it was on point tonight and the dishes kept us from talking much.

"I've told you what you need to know. And you know that we're going to have fun," he answers with a smirk.

"Well duh, we always have fun," I say, rolling my eyes. I catch the change on his face for only a split second before his smirk is back. If I didn't know any better, I would think he just grimaced.

I shake my head, trying to clear that thought, because what could possibly make him upset about us having fun together? I smile at him, a little wary. Is he worried about the next few days? What could he have planned?

Weston seems to sense the direction my thoughts are heading and grabs my hand, bringing it to his lips.

"What about dessert? I bought some of your favorite ice cream when I stopped at the store the other day," Wes says, kissing the back of my hand, then my palm and trailing down to my wrist. "Or I could think of something even sweeter," he growls, lifting me out of my chair like I weigh nothing at all.

By the time we make it through the threshold of his door, I've completely forgotten about the worries I was holding onto in the kitchen.

Except, "What about the dishes?" I ask, poking Weston in the chest with my finger.

"They can wait. I can't."

And just like that, every other thought besides him is pushed from my head.

≫→

"What time are we leaving? I'm packed but I want to make sure I have time to dry my hair after my shower," I say, making my way into the bathroom.

"The only plans with concrete times today don't start until 8 tonight. You have plenty of time. Dry your hair, do whatever else you need to. Don't feel like you have to rush for any of this," Weston responds from the kitchen.

He's working on cleaning up the mess from last night. We never made it back out of the bedroom and some of the pans are having to be scrubbed. I laugh, thinking about the look on his face this morning when he saw them. All he said was that it was worth every moment of last night. Which of course made me blush like crazy.

"Okay!" I shout back, knowing good and well that I'm still going to feel rushed. I decide to take a moment and try to calm myself, not wanting to make Weston nervous with my unfounded anxiety.

I step into the shower, focusing on the way the water is running over my face and letting my anxiety flow down the drain with it. I practice some of the positive affirmations that Lexa taught me in St. Croix. I tell myself that I am worthy and kind and beautiful.

"I've never heard anything more true," Weston says as he slides into the shower behind me. I can't help the smile that takes over my face as he begins to massage my scalp.

"I didn't even hear you come in. You're awfully silent for your size," I say, laughing.

"I can keep quiet when I need to. I thought you might want some help washing all this luscious hair," he replies, running his fingers through my tresses.

"Mmm, I won't stop you. That feels so good," I say, leaning back into his chest as his hands continue to knead my scalp and neck.

After probably the longest shower of my life and thanks to Weston's magical fingers, I'm more relaxed and much less anxious about this little trip. I think it's just the element of surprise that has me the most nervous. I don't know what he has planned and that makes it hard for me to feel confident in my decisions.

But every time that thought crosses my mind, Weston is there to smooth away the worry.

He left me in the bathroom to do the rest of my hair routine. As I'm drying the last of my layers, I shout out to the living room, "Do I need makeup on for tonight?"

"You know my answer to that is always going to be no. Because you're gorgeous. But if it would make you feel better, then absolutely. We will be out in public, but that's all I'm going to tell you."

"Will I have time to put makeup on before 8 if I decide I don't want to put it on now?" I ask, still trying to divine any knowledge of tonight's plans.

Weston's voice comes from the doorway as he stands there looking at me. "Yes," he answers finally. "You'll have time to do whatever you need. Like I said, we don't have any set plans until then and luckily for you, I know how long it takes you to get ready." He smiles and throws me a wink before coming forward for a quick kiss.

He grabs a handful of my ass and gives it a squeeze for good measure before saying, "If you would rather do your hair and makeup now, that's fine. But if you want to wait until we get there, that's also fine. Either way, I get you all to myself for the next several days.

I laugh and lean up to kiss him, making sure to slip some tongue in there before pulling away. His eyes darken with promise and desire but he lets me get back to getting ready.

"I think I'll just throw my hair up in a clip to save the blow out and do my makeup once we get there. Wherever *there* is," I say, shooting another glance his way. Still no hints of what lay in wait for tonight.

"Sounds like a plan to me. Does that mean you're ready to head out?" Weston asks, hope coloring his voice.

"Indeed, my good sir. Are you ready?" I ask, giving him a once over full of anticipation. He reads the look on my face and with a light growl he pulls me forward, locking me against his chest.

"I've been ready, my dear," he answers, not letting me move from his side.

It's hard not to read into his statement, whether he's been

looking forward to this exact time in our relationship for a long time, or if he really just means he's been sitting on the couch and ready to go.

Either way, I'm just along for the ride at this point. I stopped trying to contain my feelings, but I'm still not to the precipice of pronouncing them to the world yet. So I'll settle for a little time to ourselves outside of our apartment and see where that leads.

Chapter 32

Weston

I can't seem to take my hand off of Grace or keep my thoughts from wandering to her the entire ride. The anticipation for this trip is killing me, but especially for tonight. I can't wait to see her reaction to my first surprise.

The amount of heat rolling off of her at the apartment guarantees this trip will be something special. While we're not going too far away from our current home-base, we're leaving the city and sometimes that's all it takes to feel like you're in your own world. I wanted her to have some new experiences while we were in Oregon, so that's what we're doing.

The restaurant we have reservations at tonight is a Michelin star affair with all the trappings of a fancy ass dinner. I know she didn't bring anything to wear for it, because I didn't tell her to. I have her outfit with me.

But before we even get to the wining and dining portion of the night, I have some fun things planned around the city. There's an art museum that I know she'll go crazy for and a cat cafe. We're going to be having a casual day out and hopefully not stuff our bellies too much before the big meal tonight.

I called ahead to the hotel and our room is ready so we'll be able to check in as soon as we get there. I'm glad that Grace is so low maintenance when it comes to getting out of the house. I love that she was happy to throw her hair up in a clip and go sans makeup for the daytime. I love being able to see the freckles dotting her tan cheeks. But I also know that she'll go all out for tonight and damn if I don't love that just as much. She takes pride in her appearance but doesn't fight against her own beauty.

I look at Grace as we pull up to the front of the hotel that I have booked for the next two nights. Her jaw drops for a second before she realizes that I'm staring at her. She closes her mouth, fixing a smile into place before saying, "We're staying here?"

"Here" is a 5 star hotel with all the amenities and the gilded gold entrance one associates with new money wealth. I don't tell her that they were running a special for healthcare workers this month and it's not nearly as pricey as it looks. I'm enjoying the shock on her face too much.

"Nothing but the best for you," I say, giving her a smile and small wink.

She reaches over to smack my arm, but I catch her hand and press a kiss to her knuckles. "Now, now dear. We don't want to seem uncivilized."

"Oh shut up," she laughs.

I wrap her hand in mine, enjoying the warmth radiating from her skin. I watch as her face lights up, taking in the scene around her. There are obvious newlyweds checking in at the desk, girl groups in the lobby talking about dinner plans and an older couple sitting by the bar and chatting. The lobby looks just as opulent as the exterior, but without all of the gold. There are rich silks strung on the walls behind the deep mahogany desks, real leather chairs and a grand fireplace. It somehow feels fancy and cozy at the same time.

Echoing my thoughts, Grace says, "This place feels like a nicer version of a home. It's weird. I don't feel uncomfortable, but I feel uptown. It's so odd."

I laugh and murmur my agreement, gently pulling her to the reservation desk.

Once we reach the counter, I hand over my license and open the email for the confirmation number. I checked in ahead of time, but I want to make sure my prior requests were honored.

"Mr. Anders? Everything is ready for you and your room has been stocked according to your wishes." The attendant smiles at me, but her smile grows exponentially wider when she meets Grace's eyes. "Have a great stay, you two. And keep us abreast of any developing needs or wants. Our front desk is staffed 24/7."

We nod our thanks and turn in unison to the bank of elevators to the right. We each hand over our weekend bags to the porter waiting at our sides. "Right this way," she says, placing our bags onto a trolley and ushering us towards the waiting car.

"Oh, thank you," Grace says, blushing.

I look down at her, watching her mouth quirk from side to side. "I thought you weren't uncomfortable? Your facial expression begs to differ," I say.

Grace just shoots me a look, one I take to mean "we'll talk about this upstairs," and follows the porter into the elevator. Once we reach our floor, we're escorted to our room where the porter asks for our key card.

We're let into our suite and I exchange the key for a tip and a thank you to our porter. She reiterates the sentiment from the front desk attendant concerning 24-hour needs. We thank her and close the door, turning to each other. I smile at Grace and then watch her face as she turns to take in the room. It takes my eyes a moment to redirect, but once they do I'm presented with the biggest and most elegant hotel suite I have ever seen.

The first thing you see as you walk in are giant floor to ceiling windows along the back wall. The sunlight streaming through lights up the living room and kitchen, showing off the stainless steel appliances and deep cushioned couch. I pull myself away from the foyer long enough to investigate the bedroom. I'm the first to the door and when I open it, I'm glad to see the champagne bottle and chocolate covered strawberries that I pre-ordered. There are gorgeous flower arrangements on the nightstands and the fluffiest duvet on the bed.

"Oh man," I say, feigning disappointment, "there's only one bed. I guess we'll have to share." It helps that I know that's her favorite romance novel trope.

Grace lets out a loud guffaw from behind me but sobers as she takes in the room. "Weston, this is gorgeous. I can't believe you booked this place for us."

"For us," I say, taking her hand in mine and placing a lingering kiss to her knuckles.

≫→

After checking to make sure the bed was as comfortable as it looked and draining a bottle of champagne, I mention the museums in the area.

Grace rolls over to face me, running her finger down my chest. "Can you read my mind? There's no way you can know me this well."

"I will say, living with you does give me a pretty decent

insight into your mind. But mostly, I just listen when you talk."

"Imagine that. I don't think you realize how rare of a quality that is nowadays," she murmurs, not pulling her eyes from the path of her finger as it grazes over my stomach.

As her fingers scorch my already overheating skin, I tuck her to my side before rolling her onto her back. I swallow the rest of her words, along with more than a few moans.

Chapter 33

Grace

With my body sated and my mind numbed to everything not Weston, I peel myself from the hotel sheets and make my way to the bathroom. A quick shower, and then we'll be on our way to the museums.

I meant what I said, Wes really does listen and seems to know me better than I even know myself. I never would have chosen this hotel, mainly because of the opulence, but I'm in love with him. *Shit.* I mean the hotel. I'm in love with the hotel. Wes and I are just....friends, right? Friends with benefits. Who happen to be faking a relationship. A little too well. But still, it's fake. I can't let myself forget that.

I shake my head, trying to clear the thoughts now running wild. I need to settle back down and return to my afterglow mindset. Just being happy and worry-free.

Throwing my hair into a loose bun with a claw clip, I turn on the shower. I step into the warm water, letting it flow over my arms and legs. I rub my arms, allowing the warmth to soak into my skin and relax the muscles there. The body wash here is actually nice and not grainy, a huge bonus. It doesn't take long before I feel clean and refreshed. Stepping out of the shower, I wrap up in an overly fluffy towel, luxuriating in the feel. I glance in the mirror and see Weston watching me from the bedroom. I smile, unable to contain the happiness that I feel when I think of him.

Once I'm in my casual tourist clothes once again—hair combed back into some semblance of order—I throw a smile over my shoulder at Weston. "Ready buddy?"

"Always, *buddy*," Wes replies, smacking my butt as he walks past.

I squeal in response but can't help the redness creeping across my cheeks.

>>+

We're into the second hall of the museum before I realize we haven't even spoken since we got here. But not in an uncomfortable silence type of way. Just walking through the galleries and looking at gorgeous, life-changing art while holding the hand of my best friend. I couldn't imagine a better way to spend the day.

"Not really your thing I know, but these are amazing. Thank you for bringing me here," I say, turning to face Weston as he studies the piece in front of us.

"My 'thing' is hanging out with you. If you're happy, I'm happy. I can appreciate beauty when I see it," Wes says, winking at me with the last part. I blush again, almost on command. Wes just chuckles and squeezes my hand. "Just so you know, this isn't the only thing I have planned today. I think you might enjoy the next stop even more than this one."

"Are you just trying to get me moving again?" I ask, laughing.

"Of course not. If we leave, I can't enjoy the view of you walking in front of me. Especially your face lighting up at the beauty surrounding you. It's almost torture really. By all means, continue the harassment."

I can't stop the laugh that bubbles from my lips, or the hand that reaches out to smack Weston's chest.

He catches my hand, kissing my palm before laying it back on his chest. Right over his heart. I can't miss the blatant emotion in his eyes and it takes everything in me not to spill my guts to him in this museum.

Instead, I turn from the temptation, swaying my hips a little more than necessary before saying, "Well let's keep moving then. Wouldn't want to miss out on the next part of our day."

➺

The second surprise? Even better than the first. I'm covered with kittens, sipping from a cat-themed coffee and eating one of the best and flakiest croissants I've ever had. The kittens are trying their hardest to get a taste of the coffee, the little fiends.

I haven't stopped smiling since we walked in and my cheeks are almost aching. This has to be what heaven consists of. Cats and coffee.

At this point, I really can't imagine this day getting any better. But knowing Weston, this is only the beginning. If I've ever known someone that's prone to going over the top, it's the gorgeous man sitting across from me, laughing as kittens climb over him like a jungle gym.

"I didn't know you were a cat person," I say, scratching a particularly loving gray tabby behind his ears. The purr I receive resonates deep in my soul.

"I love animals, but I've never had a cat. We always had

dogs growing up. These little things are great, though." The smile hasn't left his face and his eyes are round like a kid's at Christmas.

"We weren't allowed to have indoor animals when I was young. I've always wanted a cat. Mainly because they don't demand to be walked in the snow and rain," I say with a laugh.

"We should get one. I've heard that they're not that hard to travel with. And most of the places we stay allow pets. We'd just have to check before we book."

When I don't respond, Weston finally looks at me. His eyebrows scrunch in confusion at the expression on my face. "What? Did I say something wrong?"

"What happened to settling down? We can't get a shared animal if we're not planning on traveling together after the wedding," I remind him.

"We can talk about it. I'm still undecided, I guess. I'm...not as ready to stop traveling as I thought," he replies, eyes back on the cats.

I can't read his thoughts when his face is hidden like this. I just inwardly sigh and continue playing with the cats. I'm not ready for this conversation yet. The thought of being separated from Weston while on assignment sounds horrible. Feels terrible. And I'm not ready to admit why, yet.

Instead, I put on a happy little smile and pick up one of the more gregarious kittens. "Maybe this one wants to come home with us," I say, trying to keep a teasing note in my near-quivering voice. The orange tabby chooses that moment to leap from my hands directly onto the head of an older black cat that had been circling my feet. A scuffle ensues, drawing laughs from Weston and myself—effectively diffusing the tension that had crept in.

"Are you getting hungry for dinner? We're eating at eight. That gives us a little time to head back to the hotel and freshen up. Or whatever else we can come up with to occupy some time...," Weston says with a wolfish wink.

"Okay Casanova, let's head out," I reply, laughter freeing the last tie of the knot in my chest.

Chapter 34

Grace

"What do you mean close my eyes and hold out my hands? I mean, it's not really a secret what's in your boxers anymore," I say, scrunching my nose in confusion.

"First of all, I'm not that perverted. Second of all, our dinner is a little nicer than I led on, and we have reservations at eight," Weston says from in front of me.

I fight every instinct yelling at me to open my eyes and see what the hell is going on. I remain seated on the bed, legs crossed at the ankle and arms outstretched. My palms are cupped, not sure what I'm expected to receive. I feel Weston's hands grip mine and gently pull my wrists apart, leaving them to rest face up and about a foot away from each other. I wiggle my fingers with impatience, pulling a chuckle from Weston.

"Is it wrong if I say I like you like this? Hip height and begging?" Weston asks, his voice darkening and causing the nerves in my core to short circuit.

I lick my lips in a tease before answering, "Just give it to me already." I put all of the seduction I can muster in those six words. Judging from the sharp intake of breath, it affected Weston in just the way I'd hoped. I wiggle my fingers again and feel the brush of satin against my palms before the weight of the fabric covers my forearms.

"Okay, open up," Weston says with another chuckle.

My eyes fly open and I gasp as I behold the most beautiful green silk in my arms. I slide the fabric down one arm until I can hold the hanger and I realize instantly that this is the other dress I tried on at the boutique last week. The forest green A-line that Weston was salivating over. My gaze leaves the dress and meets Weston's searching eyes.

"You...bought me the other dress?" I ask, unable to break our stare.

"I couldn't leave it behind after seeing it on you. It was made for you. I thought you might want to wear it tonight. We're going to that fancy ass restaurant down the street and I didn't tell you to pack anything for it. I brought shoes, too," he says, pulling my nude pumps from behind his back.

"Oh, Wes," is all I can say. I can feel the pressure behind my eyes, the tears starting to well up on my lashes. This is so—"So incredibly thoughtful."

"Oh, it's nothing really. You needed this dress and I needed an excuse to see you in it again," he hedges. The sheepish smile on his face is killing me. I gently lay the dress down on the bed before leaping into his arms. He catches me, just as I knew he would. That's what friends are for right...to be there to catch you when you fall. Too bad I'm falling for him and I don't know if that's a catch he's willing to make.

➤➤

"Weston Anders," I hiss as soon as we're seated. "This place is way too nice. What were you thinking? You already got the room. I'm getting this."

"Absolutely not. This is a date and I'm paying. End of discussion. Now look over this list with me and help me pick a wine. You're better at it than I am." The authority in his voice does things to me and I have to ignore the sudden ache between my legs. I shift and recross my legs but catch the knowing smirk on Weston's face as I look up.

"Let's do a glass of champagne for a toast to begin? Then when we order, we can pick our wine. How does that sound?"

Weston's gaze is fixed on my mouth when he replies, "Perfect."

I can't help the smile that stretches my lips. I am, however, fully in control of the small bite I apply to my bottom lip. Weston's tongue darts out to catch his lower lip like he's soothing my marks from across the table. I lean in and press a soft kiss to his mouth, pulling back before I get lost.

"Maybe dinner was a bad idea," he says, voice husky with hunger for something other than food. His eyes are so dark, his pupils have swallowed the color of his iris.

"Why is that?" I ask, letting my hand fall onto his knee.

"Because I can't touch you how I want to right now. It feels like torture," he says, leaning into my touch and kissing me again.

"Well, we need some sustenance before we engage in any further *touching* tonight, I'd say."

"You're right. Let's load up on carbs and then go work it off," Wes says, laughing with a low and breathy chuckle.

"Incorrigible."

Chapter 35

Weston

It's getting harder and harder for me to play this as fake. The way Grace makes me come alive doesn't feel fake. And I hope she doesn't think the way I look at her is in any way pretend. I can't stop looking at her, getting close to her and smiling at her. She's it.

The way she looks in that green silk is doing things to my head. And other areas. It's taking everything in me not to suggest she head to the restroom just so I can follow her in there. This place is way too fancy-schmancy for a bathroom hook-up and Grace looks too nice for me to mess anything up tonight. But as soon as we get back to the room, all bets are off.

We're finally to the dessert course, a tiramisu with a glass of sweet red wine. I'm trying my best to eat and drink slowly, but the way that dress is hugging her figure is sinful.

Grace's eyes lift slowly to my face, taking in my surely ravenous look. "See something you like?" she teases, before forking up another bite of the tiramisu and offering it to me.

"I could think of something that would taste even better dusted with espresso…," I say, winking.

She gasps and has to drink some wine to clear her throat of said coffee coating. "Um…eww?"

"I was thinking chocolate covered strawberries…what were you thinking?" I ask, playing innocent. It works because Grace's cheeks immediately turn bright red and she splutters on the next sip of wine.

"Oh you naughty, naughty girl," I tease, my voice dipping low to keep this conversation at our table. "Whatever could you have been imagining?"

"Shut up. You know exactly where you were leading me with that statement. You've had your bedroom eyes on me since we sat down," she whispers.

"It was before that, I believe. Probably since we left the bedroom. You don't know what you're doing to me in that dress."

A pretty blush steals across her cheekbones again, accenting the sparkle in her dark eyes. "Well, it looks like we're done with dessert. How about we settle this bill and go somewhere a little more…private," Grace says, running her foot along the outside of my calf. She makes it up to my knee before I have to grab her ankle under the table.

"Don't start something you're not willing to finish right here, *buddy.*"

Her eyes turn pitch black with need, churning the desire already building to a boiling point in me. I see our waiter out of the corner of my eye and discreetly motion for the check. I already have my card out and ready, handing it over as soon as our waiter reaches us.

"Be right back, sir," he says. Grace and I don't break eye

contact long enough to acknowledge the statement. With my hand still wrapped around her bare ankle, I run my thumb over the pulse point on the inside of her foot and feel the pounding of her heart.

"Here you go, you two have a great night and we hope to see you again soon," our waiter says, setting the folio down on the table with my card inside. Leaving my occupied hand where it is, I flip open the little leather book, tip and sign. I stuff my card into my wallet with my free hand and within seconds, I'm on my feet and pulling Grace's chair out.

"Milady," I say, gesturing towards the door.

She snorts before taking my hand and pulling me with her. "Let's go. I'm ready to get you out of those ass-hugging pants. Where did you even find those? I've never seen a pair of dress pants fit someone like that before."

"I actually got them tailored. They fit so well in the thighs and butt, I figured I might as well get them fitted to my waist. I do that with a lot of my pants actually. It's easier than cinching a belt as tight as it will go," I reply, shrugging.

"God, you're such an adult. I want to be you when I grow up," Grace says, a touch of wistfulness entering her voice.

I lean in to whisper, "I want to be *in you* when I grow up." I watch with satisfaction as a shiver runs down Grace's body and laugh as her deep gaze swivels back to meet mine.

"I can't believe you just said that."

"But you love that I did," I state, knowing it's the truth. Grace just sighs, shrugging as if she can't argue.

The elevator trip to the room is one of the most tense rides of my life. There's an older couple sharing our car and I know they can feel the sexual tension pouring from my veins. When the door opens and we get out on our floor, I swear I hear them sigh with relief behind us.

But when the door to our room finally opens, it's game over. We don't even bother with a light before I'm pulling that sexy green silk over Grace's head and she's ripping at the buttons of my shirt.

I spin us around, pushing her up against the wall by the door and begin to thoroughly explore her mouth. The moans I'm pulling from her are devastating to my self-control. Before I know it, I'm on my knees in front of my girl, her hands fisted in my hair while she calls my name like a prayer.

Chapter 36

Grace

We wake to the soft patter of rain against the glass of the windows. The morning light is still strong enough that it's streaming through the curtains we forgot to close before we fell asleep. To be fair, our minds were a little preoccupied with other things.

I feel the full body exhaustion of a wonderful night spent with Weston. The way he devours me as he worships my body is truly magnificent. I'm afraid at this point that I'm ruined for anyone else. Not that I even want anyone else. Ever. Ugh, what is this man doing to me? We're in a fake relationship with very real sex and I'm having very real feelings. I'm going to get my heart broken and I'm powerless to even try to save myself.

I stretch like a cat, rolling over to face Weston. I crack my eyes open to see that he's already awake, and watching me.

"Well, good morning beautiful," he murmurs, pulling me into his chest.

"Good morning. You don't look so bad yourself," I reply, wrapping my legs up in his.

Weston drops his lips down onto my forehead, giving me a gentle kiss. Then he's onto my nose, then each cheek before finally landing on my mouth. He tortures me with a slow, sweet kiss, acting like we have all the time in the world to do just this. I startle slightly when I realize that we do. We have all day.

"What are the plans for today?" I ask, pulling back but placing a kiss to the tip of Weston's nose for good measure.

"I have a bit of a surprise. It involves ordering in some breakfast, maybe even lunch. We won't have to get out in the rain, and you can dress—or undress—however you want," he says, reaching down to cup my bare ass in emphasis.

"Sounds perfect to me. What part of that is the surprise though?" I ask, already thinking about getting some coffee ordered up.

"Oh, you'll see. Don't worry."

With some nervous energy surging through my body, I shiver and smile. The anticipation of a surprise from Weston is enough to keep me more than mildly curious. If last night is any indication, he has some big plans for today.

I never intended to be so thoroughly wined and dined—I've never had a guy wanting to go to this much trouble for me. And just knowing that Weston is capable of this type of relationship is making it harder and harder to keep going through with the fake dating thing. I'm going to end up majorly hurt at the end of this, but it's worth it just to see what I *could be* experiencing if I would raise my dating standards. And that is going to have to be my main takeaway from all of this. If Weston can treat me this well as a friend, I don't deserve to be treated any less by a partner.

With every kind word and thoughtful gesture, Wes has instilled an unheard of amount of confidence in me. I have never felt more sure of myself than when I'm seeing myself through Weston's eyes.

Trying to keep that idea in my mind, I rise from bed and walk to the bathroom, allowing a little strut to enter my walk. I have no reason to cover myself in front of him, he's already seen—and thoroughly touched—everything.

"I think I'm going to take a quick shower. Ooh, or maybe a bath. They have bubbles in here and a bath bomb," I call over my shoulder, noting that Weston hasn't moved from the bed, nor taken his eyes off of me.

"Sounds good to me, sweetness. I'm going to call down and get breakfast ordered. Anything in particular you're wanting?" Weston's eyes darken with the word *want*, but he doesn't make a move to follow me into the bathroom.

"Pancakes, please! And coffee. Don't forget the coffee!" I turn the water on, running my hand under the stream until the heat is perfect. I press the stopper in and gather my materials near the edge of the tub in preparation for a nice bath.

I slip into the luxuriously scented water, letting the bubbles wash over my skin. I let out a groan, feeling the immediate relaxation of my tender muscles. I'm not as used to walking in heels as I once was and my calves are aching a bit from last night. Among other well-loved parts of my body, that is.

I can't imagine anything better at this moment. My eyes drift closed as the eucalyptus scent of the bath bomb floods my senses. I hear a small shuffle near the door and open my eyes to see Weston handing me a glass of orange juice. I smile in thanks before taking a sip of what I quickly realize is a mimosa. The bubbles from the champagne tingle on my tongue and I savor the sensation before taking another, more prepared sip.

"Thought you might want something to keep you cooled

off in this steamy bath," he says, bowing low in his gray sweatpants as he exits the bathroom.

I laugh at his absurdity. He's just so thoughtful, bringing me something to drink while I'm choosing to pamper myself. Other guys would be pouting that I either didn't invite them, or that I'm not choosing to spend all of my time with them. I guess it's mainly because Weston and I are still just friends. Through all of this—just friends.

I let my mind wander, trying and failing to forget about whatever surprise awaits me after breakfast.

The water is starting to cool by the time I feel ready to get out. I pull the stopper and step out onto the soft bath rug. After drying off, I pull a plush hotel robe on, cinching it around my waist. As I wander towards the bedroom, I hear Weston speaking with the hotel staff at the front door. Then the sounds of metal and porcelain mix with the smells of maple syrup and bacon. My stomach doesn't hesitate before letting out a loud growl. I chuckle and follow my nose into the dining area.

I put a hand over my stomach to silence the growling and let out a gasp when I see the spread on the table. Pancakes, bacon, cinnamon rolls, eggs, salmon bagels and three different types of juices cover the glass surface.

"Weston, you did not have to do all of this," I say, stepping towards him with a disbelieving smile on my face.

"Well, you're going to need some fuel so I figured I'd make sure you got enough this morning. And then we can order lunch in, too. Whatever you like," Wes says, reaching forward to grab my hands, pulling me closer.

His hands drop down to my waist as his mouth finds mine.

"Good morning again, gorgeous," he breathes against my lips, before taking my lower lip in between his teeth. With a soft nibble, he has me melting against him.

Chapter 37

Weston

It takes every bit of self-control that I possess to release Grace. If I wasn't so nervous about this surprise that I have planned, I would scoop her up and take her right back to the bedroom. But, I want her to eat a good breakfast before we spend the rest of the day...not eating.

I slip my hands under the tie of her robe, letting my thumbs run along her rib cage and to the underside of her breasts. She shivers in my arms and I smile as I press a kiss to the top of her head.

"Okay, food," I laugh. I pull my hands from her warm body and cinch her robe back together, trying to remove the temptation to just take it off.

Grace just giggles before turning back to the breakfast buffet assembled on the table. I fight back a groan as she licks those plump lips of hers. My voice is a little too gravelly as I say, "Eat up, buttercup. Whatever you want."

Grace darts toward the pancakes with a speed I would have never imagined that she possessed. I laugh as she then smothers the stack in syrup before reaching back down to pop a cinnamon roll onto her plate. With a final flourish of bacon, she looks ready to sit down.

"What are the juices?" she asks, gesturing to the carafes by the centerpiece.

"Pineapple, orange and cranberry. I thought we'd have a little variety to mix with our champagne."

"How wonderful. That will also cover my fruit intake, since I don't have any room on my plate for a serving, anyway," she says with a bright smile.

Dammit. I knew I was forgetting something. She must catch the look on my face because she adds, "If I'm going to need protein and fuel for whatever you have planned for today, I don't want fruit. I want this." She sweeps a hand over her full plate and gives me a sweet and sincere smile.

"Well, I knew you were a meats and sweets girl. I thought this would be appropriate," I wink, trying to keep myself level. I feel like I'm on the verge of crawling out of my skin. She's either going to love the surprise or think I've gone insane. Maybe both. I just need to get through breakfast and then we can get started.

Grace sinks into the plush velvet chair across from the spread, leaving the one at the head of the table for me. I watch as she starts to dig into her pancakes, strangling a groan as syrup lines her lips. All I can think about is licking it off.

I carry a glass of champagne over to her, gesturing to the juice setup in the middle. "What will it be, madam?" I ask, swooping low to place a kiss on her hairline.

She deliberates for a moment, hand touching her chin in a contemplative gesture. "Hmm, could I try some cranberry *and* some pineapple? I feel like that might be yummy."

"Of course, madam. What a wonderful selection. How wise you are," I reply with a bow.

She snickers and stuffs some bacon in her mouth to cut off what probably would have been a very sarcastic response.

I top off her drink with the requested juices, taking a sip to test the concoction. "Mmm, very good. Here you should try it."

She doesn't try to contain the guffaw that erupts from her throat, basically swiping the drink from my hand. "Give that here!"

I laugh along with her, then watch as her throat bobs with the sip before her tongue peeks out to lick her lips. Everything she does should not be this attractive to me, but here we are.

I settle into my chair, taking a sip of my own cranberry mimosa and watch Grace for a few more minutes. She swings around slightly in her chair, resting her feet in my lap. I instinctively reach down and start massaging one. I smile to myself as soon as I catch the fact that my natural reaction is to take care of this woman.

We eat in companionable silence, both silently stealing glances at each other.

I don't know if she can feel the tension in my body, but she feels nice and relaxed. Maybe my brain will take a cue and calm down, too.

Breakfast ends up being a longer meal that I thought it would. Neither of us seem to be in any particular hurry. That is, until Grace finishes her last piece of bacon. She quickly pulls her feet from my lap and leans forward on the table. "So, about this surprise...," she says, resting her chin on her clasped hands.

"Oh that? You're ready now, are you?"

Grace blushes slightly before saying, "I mean, if you are."

It's now or never Weston, come on. I push back from the table quickly, trying not to lose my nerve. "Stay right there for just a second. And uh, close your eyes," I say, a little too gruffly. But I'm on the verge of calling this off at the last second.

"Yes sir," Grace says with a smile on her face. Her delicately formed hands are covering her eyes and I take just a second to admire the beautiful curve to her lips and the gentle sweep of her nose. She's so damn gorgeous.

"And keep them closed," I say, more gently this time. "No matter what you hear me doing in here, just keep 'em covered, buddy."

I work quickly, moving things that I had hidden behind the sofa. There's only one big item, the rest are easily put into place. And then it's my turn. I exhale a steadying breath and get into position.

I take one more fortifying breath, squeezing my eyes closed to shore up some courage before slowly blowing it back out.

"Okay Grace, open your eyes."

Chapter 38

Grace

I gasp, my hands moving from my eyes to my mouth. My brain can't seem to form words but my lips are trying.

The scene laid out in front of me is as magnificent as it is unexpected. There's a brand new easel set up in the center of the living room, with a large sketch pad and a table placed beside it. On the table there are new pencils, charcoal and paint, new brushes and a new palette. But the most spectacular part? Weston. Sprawled across a white blanket, basking in the morning glow of the sun, completely nude. My breath leaves me in a whoosh, as though I've been hit in the gut.

I can't contain the smile taking over my mouth. Weston is looking right at me, a sensuous promise on his lips, every muscle on display in a delicious buffet for the eyes.

My body begins to move before I realize I've even decided to get up. I make my way over to the couch, touching my subject to get a feel for the curves I'll be depicting.

"This is…," I start, unable to finish as my eyes once again meet his.

"I thought you might want to have a full picture. I may have seen your sketches of me the last several months, but they're all bits and pieces. I know you have your own supplies, too. I wanted to make sure you had enough. And you had been talking about wanting to try charcoal so...," I put a finger to his lips, halting the flow of his words.

"This is perfect. Thank you. Though I am a little embarrassed that you found my stash of drawings of you, I'm not that surprised. I'd gotten a little careless with where I left it. Are you sure you're ready? This is going to be hours of me looking at you, touching you and you having to lay in this position. I will feed you during some breaks, however."

"Paint me like one of your French boys," Weston replies with a roguish wink.

I laugh loudly, calming enough to say, "Alright then. Let's get started. I'm loving this lighting on you and I want to capture as much of this as I can."

"Yes ma'am. I am but a muse, I will do as you command." Wes winks again.

"God you're corny," I say, walking back to the easel and starting to open the pencils. I check the points, correcting some with the sharpener and dulling a few to begin. I'll save the paint for later. I want to go ahead and get this sketched out with the shadows as they are now.

Weston relaxes back into his pose as my hand finds the paper. I begin sketching, looking between him and the page, utterly absorbed in the process. This is so much better than drawing scraps of him from memory or trying to subtly capture bits of him while we're together. I get a full picture of Weston forever and I have never been more happy.

Hours pass in this haze of beauty. Weston keeps his promise

and doesn't move from his spot, no matter what I'm doing. I take advantage of his stillness and use the time to trace the muscles of his abs with my fingers, delicately outlining each dip and curve with my hand. While it does make it easier to sketch, it's also just nice to touch him like this.

"Do you touch all of your live models this way?" Weston asks, my fingertips playing over the hair at the base of his abdomen.

I grin devilishly before replying, "Wouldn't you like to know."

His mouth flattens into a line, but he still doesn't move his body. It's this, among other things about him that make me fall even more for him. Even frustrated with me, he doesn't break a promise.

"No, I don't," I finally tell him. "Mainly because you're the only live model I have ever had to actually sit for me."

"I thought you'd been sketching forever? No one in your family ever sat for you?"

"Well, no. My grandparents encouraged my art, but they weren't willing to take time out of their day like that. Not to say that I didn't still draw them every chance I got. Like I've done with you. Pieces of memory and small bits of time."

"Damn Grace. I really like this. I'll sit for you anytime," Wes says, a gentleness to his voice.

"I think you just like being touched," I tease, running my hand over his pecs, across his ribs and down his hip.

Weston shivers slightly in response before saying, "Well, it is definitely a perk of the job."

We both laugh and I stand to return to the easel. I feel my stomach grumble slightly and realize it might be time for a little break. I veer to the table where remnants of breakfast are still laid out. I grab a cinnamon roll and some bacon. Heading back to the couch, I feed Weston some bacon and break off some pieces of the roll. He smiles, letting me feed him while his hands remain above his head in his lounging position.

"Yeah," he laughs, "I could get used to this."

The sun has moved from one side of the wall of windows to the other by the time I'm finishing up the background painting. I'm glad I got my shading in with the morning sun, the shadows on Weston make him look much less angelic at this time of day. If anything, he looks like my own personal devil.

A little thrill runs through me, thinking of just how *bad* he can be.

"What's that smile for, buddy? You look like you've got a secret," Weston says, still lounging and on full display.

"Just thinking about you, *buddy*," I reply, leaning fully around the easel to glance suggestively at what he has to offer.

"Oh really? Well I am fully intent on punishing you a bit for all of this sitting still while you've gotten to touch me. We'll see how much you're smiling then."

I gasp, my face heating under his scorching glare.

I return my attention to my work, noticing that I only have one area of shading left and then I'll be done. It's not perfect by any means, but I love it and I hope Weston does, too.

A few more swipes of the charcoal and I sit back, looking over the page to make sure I haven't missed anything.

"How's it looking?" he asks.

"Well, not as good as the real thing," I reply with a wink towards the subject, "but it's done. I think."

"Do I get to see or am I to remain in this position?"

I look him over and decide there's something I want to do

right now. Before he even sees what we've been working on.

I walk slowly over the couch, not letting my eyes leave his. "You can see it, but there's something I've been looking forward to all day. So I'll need you to stay in that position for just a bit longer." I finally let my eyes drop, eyeing my target. I sink to my knees beside the couch and say, "Now keep those hands right where they are."

"Yes ma'am," Weston says before a sharp inhale steals his ability to talk.

Chapter 39

Weston

After Grace kills me *oh so slowly*, I finally get to move from my position on the couch. And I take full advantage of that immediately. I move Grace down to the floor, returning the favor. I edge her several times before finally letting her release. She deserves it for all of the touching when I couldn't.

We lay on the floor for a while before I hear her stomach grumbling. We skipped lunch and I'm going to need some food in her before we spend the rest of our night getting in some physical activity.

"Hungry?" I ask, letting my hand drift to her stomach. I run a finger over her ribs and circle her peaked nipple before I give her a pinch. She jerks against me before slapping my hand away.

"Yes, I'm starved. Want to order some food or do you want to go out?" she asks, holding my hand in hers.

"Oh buddy, we're not leaving this room. And neither of us are getting any more dressed than we already are," I reply, my voice growing husky as my eyes take in the delicious woman beside me.

She blushes and I trace the color from her cheeks down her neck before planting a kiss at the curve of her collarbone.

"Well," she replies, "let's get some food ordered and then you can check out the work I did. See if you approve or not."

I wish I couldn't hear the slight nervousness in her voice. There's no reason for her to be anxious. She knows I think she's incredible.

"I can't wait to see it," I say, getting up and dropping a hand to pull Grace from the floor. I tug her straight into my chest, placing a kiss on her forehead, then cheeks, then nose and finally her lips. "I'm sure it's just as amazing as you are."

We wander to the table to find the room service menu and order some grub. Once our meal is handled, Grace turns to me, suddenly bashful. "You, um, wanna see it?" she asks.

"Of course. Lead the way," I reply, taking her hand and placing a kiss to her palm before clasping it in mine.

She gives me the sweetest smile, laced with hope and turns back to the living room. Of course, I could have just looked at the portrait as we were leaving the room earlier, but that wasn't the deal. I was waiting until it was unveiled for me. And getting to watch Grace as she does so, makes any wait worth it. Her face is lit from within, her smile taking over her cheeks. There's a gleam in her eye that I haven't seen before and I recognize that it's pride in her work. She's excited to show this portrait to me and she's nervous about my reaction, but underneath it all, she's proud of herself. And that makes my heart swell. I already love everything about this woman and this is the icing on the cake.

"Okay, cover your eyes," she says, in an imitation of me from earlier in our day. I oblige immediately and let her continue to lead me toward the finished work. "Now, obviously it's not perfect, but I think it looks great. And knowing that I'll have this piece of you forever is just...," she trails off. I want so badly to peek, just to be able to read her expression right now. But I don't. My eyes stay covered and I give her hand a quick squeeze. She squeezes back and says, "Okay, open up."

I'm greeted with the most beautiful portrait I have ever seen. I can't even believe it's of me. She made me look like a damn Greek god. The light is highlighting each stretch of skin in a way that enhances muscles I know I don't have. And the eyes. I've never thought that my eyes were dull, but in her painting, they're full of so much life. And love. Damn, there's no way she can miss that right?

I'm stunned beyond words. It takes me a moment to realize that I'm standing close to the portrait, just staring. Seeing myself through Grace's eyes is a pleasure I never knew to want. She sees me in a way I have never seen myself. Where I've always hated my slightly crooked smile, she's shown it as a half-grin full of lust. My roughened hands are splayed above my head in a promise of strength.

I soak it in just a minute longer before I finally turn to Grace. "Wow. Just wow," is all I can manage.

The expression on her face is full of apprehension and it breaks my heart that she hasn't always experienced praise over her work. I take both of her hands in mine, pulling them to my mouth for a kiss to each knuckle in a silent thanks. Then I pull her into me, letting her hands fall to wrap around my waist. I kiss her fully on the lips, trying to pour every unspoken emotion into that touch. I pull away, keeping her firmly in my embrace.

"Grace," I begin, my voice quavering, "this is the most

beautiful thing I have ever seen. You have made a masterpiece out of mud and I will be forever grateful to have seen myself through your eyes. You are magnificent and this is amazing. I don't know if I even have the right words to explain what I'm feeling or to convey the magnitude of your talent. You are incredible. This is incredible."

Grace's lower lip is quivering. I swipe my thumb across it, trying to still the movement. I don't want her to cry, but I understand her need to. Instead of letting her tears start to fall, I sweep her up into my arms and carry her to our bed. Intending to show her everything I can't say.

Starting with how much I love her.

Chapter 40

Grace

Not surprisingly, we never made it out of the room yesterday. We ordered in a late lunch and then a late dinner, complete with some strawberries and whipped cream. It was a perfect night.

I'm afraid for our "back to reality" moment that will come when we get back to the apartment in a half an hour.

I notice that Weston seems just as much in his head. We've been quiet since we left the hotel. Not an awkward silence, just content. His hand is firmly wrapped around mine and he strokes my thumb every once in a while.

We're on the road for our apartment by the time I get up the nerve to finally ask, "So do we just go back to normal life? Because that's not how these last two days felt. They felt like… more. More than just a pretend relationship. More than just putting on an act for your family."

Weston is quiet for a moment, still stroking his thumb across mine. There's a new set to the curve of his lips, like he's deep in thought. Or worried.

"Let's grab some coffee before we go back to the apartment," he says. I don't miss that he's completely avoiding the question, but I'm not willing to call him on it. I can't put myself out there any more than I just did with my question.

I feel like my heart is near stopping as we roll up to the curb near the coffee shop. I follow Weston's lead, walking into the cafe while he holds open the door. We order and sit down at an open table in the corner. I don't really know what we're doing here and I'm feeling more and more like this is a weird way to breakup with someone. Like we live together, at least until the end of this contract. He could have told me in the car that he's fine just staying friends with all of these benefits. Or maybe he's tired of all of it. He's tired of even having to pretend to date me and he's calling it off altogether. Maybe he thinks we're close enough to real now that we can just stop and his family will still believe it.

I'm so far into my own head, I don't realize Weston has started talking. He apparently noticed my lack of attention, too. Because he's now reaching across the table, grabbing my hand and dipping his eyes to meet my gaze.

"Back with me, buddy?" Weston asks. I smile, meeting his eyes and inhaling when I see how molten brown and golden they are.

I open my mouth to reply in the affirmative—and maybe add to whatever conversation we're having here—but the barista calls out the names on our order. Weston releases my hand and walks to the counter. I can't help but notice the look the beautiful woman behind the bar gives Wes, but he doesn't seem to. Before she can even finish her full smile, he's turned back around.

Weston sets my latte in front of me, blowing across the rim

of his mug. "Okay, ready to try that again? I'm not sure where you were, but I don't think you were hearing anything coming out of my mouth."

"Yes," I say with a tight smile. "I'm ready. Go ahead and say what you were going to say. I'm ready." I inhale and hold it. I'm too nervous to breathe.

"Breathe Grace. Just breathe. I don't need you passing out at this table."

"Okay, sorry. Go ahead. I'm breathing. I'm being normal," I say, trying for another smile.

"Normal? Okay, I'll believe that when I see it. Anyway, all I was asking was what brought up that question in the car," Weston says, putting me right back in the hot seat.

"Oh. Um, well, it's just...," I start, not sure where I'm going.

"Are you not happy right now? Do you want more? Do you want less? That's what we're here to talk about," he says, ever so gently.

I huff out a sigh, unsure why I can't just say what I want. Weston always seems so sure of himself and his feelings. "I want what we have. I don't want less. But I don't know what more means. But I don't want less, I know that. I don't want to go back to how this started with a hookup on the down-low. We're already sleeping in your bed and going on dates. That's enough for me," I say, leaving out the *for now.*

I'm not ready to ask for more. I'm still terrified of *more* with Weston. He wants to settle down and I don't think I'm ready for that. I just know that I want him.

"Okay," Wes says with a sweet grin, "I can do that. What we have is nice. We can keep it that way." It's hard not to miss the small flicker of disappointment in his eyes, but I can't decide what it's for. Am I asking for too much or too little?

Instead of torturing myself further, I take a sip of my coffee and say, "Well great then. So when do you work again? Tomorrow?"

Weston looks at me, not missing my abrupt change in the conversation. "Yes, tomorrow. You're back tomorrow night?"

"Yep!" I reply, with far more enthusiasm than I feel over that fact. I just want to go back to that hotel room and crawl back into our little bubble and never leave.

But that's not possible and I need to get out of that mentality sooner rather than later. If not, it could end up being detrimental to my mental health. This whole situation will be, if I'm right. I still don't know what any of this means for either of us. Are we actually dating? Is this still just a ploy to help him get his family off of his back?

One thing is for sure, there's no way his family will be doubting our feelings for each other. It's hard enough for us to ignore them, though we seem to be trying our hardest.

Chapter 41

Weston

Everything slips back into place as we soon as settle into our work-life routines. We're working, spending our free time together and sleeping in the same bed. I'm still a bit unsettled about the conversation we had at the coffee house. It was hard to tell what Grace was asking me—what she wanted from me. And I was too chicken shit to push for what I wanted. If she says no to the full-blown real deal relationship that I want, it will ruin me. And I'm not ready for that. So I'll keep just doing this—this half-ass kinda-together thing that we have going on now.

Whatever she wants. I want her however I can have her. Even if that means that there's an expiration date. The wedding is next week and it's getting harder to ignore that there is a predetermined end to our time together. We haven't signed new contracts, both planning to take some time to do other things before going back to hospitals. I want to be where she is. But I don't want her to feel like I'm hanging on like a lost puppy. This is getting complicated in a way I never imagined.

"So, how was the surprise trip? We never got a chance to talk about it," Ian asks.

"It was amazing," I reply with a long sigh. We're scrubbing in for our second surgery case this morning and I've been in my head since I walked through the door.

"That sigh sounds not amazing. What's up, dude?" Ian glances over at me, concern in his eyes.

I laugh, realizing that I am way too easy to read. "It really was amazing. The whole trip was great. She's incredible and I want...more of it. I want more. But I'm terrified to even broach that with her."

"She's happy with your situation as it is?" Ian sketches a brow with some lack of belief.

"Well, I think so. When we got back, we talked about it and she seemed like this is what she wants. She said she likes that we're going on dates and spending our free time together and everything like that. And she only uses her room for the closet at this point. And even when I'm not home, she sleeps in my bed. Our bed, I guess. I don't know. I don't want to push her into something she's not ready for. She told me several months ago that she wasn't ready to settle down."

Ian finishes his scrub and turns to me with his wet hands pointed up in the air, "I think that means in life, not in a relationship. Plus dude, being with you isn't 'settling.'"

"Oh, thanks. That really means a lot, man," I say, blushing. I laugh to cover up the color rising in my face from the compliment. I know that's probably what she meant, but what if it's not?

I try my hardest to shake out of this funk and focus on the patients for the day. We have some interesting cases lined up and I want to learn and be ready for whatever. Work is the best place to get out of my own head. I used to work ER like Lexa and Ansley, but when I moved to the OR, my life changed for the better. I loved the hectic activity of the ER, but I felt stagnant. I have learned so much since I switched and my schedule is much better for my mental health. And it will be easier to help with family matters if that day ever comes for me.

There's a lull in our day when we finish a case earlier than expected. Me and Ian take the opportunity to grab something to eat and I can tell by the look on his face that he's about to talk about Grace again. Before he can even get the words out, I blurt, "Hey, so we're going to my sister's wedding in southern Cal next week, would you want to come with us? There's a lot of parties planned surrounding the wedding and it's outside. There's a buffet at the reception and my sister told me that I could bring a friend if I wanted. I don't think she's convinced that me and Grace are together and she wants me to have a buffer in case my mom acts crazy."

Ian just stuffs a few more bites of his sandwich in his mouth, chewing slowly and staring at me. "Um, what a generous offer. But, I really am not that interested in coming to get in the way of whatever is happening between you and Grace. Love you though, mean it," he finishes with a smile.

I huff, knowing he's right. I take another bite of my pasta, chewing and thinking.

"Look, man. It's okay that you're feeling all of this. And I can almost guarantee Grace is feeling the same way you are. Why don't you just talk to her?" Ian asks, ever the wise one, apparently.

"I'm too nervous. I don't want to push too far and run her off. Especially before the wedding. She's too loyal and would still come with me and try to act like my girlfriend even if we were fighting. I can't do that to her. It's not all or nothing yet. I still have some time. And maybe I can use the next week to show her how good of a real boyfriend I can be. Then she won't have anything to be scared of," I muse, twirling the noodles around my fork before shoveling the last bite into my mouth.

"Whatever you say, dude. You're the one in this messed up situation, I just don't want to see you hurt. I know we haven't known each other long, but you're a genuinely good guy."

"Aw shucks, Ian. You're gonna make me blush again," I say, my smile more teasing than anything. "But ditto. You're a great friend. Thank you for listening to all of my bullshit over the last couple of months."

"It's been my own personal reality show, so don't worry about it," he says with a laugh. "Let's head back down to the OR and start scrubbing before Karen has to come and find us."

We stand, cleaning off our area of the table and heading to the trash cans. "That lady scares the shit out of me."

"Honestly, me too," Ian says, no longer laughing.

Chapter 42

Grace

I don't know that I've ever been this anxious about someone else's wedding before. I've been in several at this point and that was much less stomach-turning than thinking about the guests at this particular wedding. I love Kiera, so it's not that. It's just the whole fake dating and being around his family as his fake girlfriend and acting like we're together—but we're not—but we *are*.

Ugh. If I didn't already have a dress for it, maybe I would just fake an illness. But I can't do that to Weston even if I wanted to. He's too precious to hurt like that. We made a deal and I'll stick to it. I've already gotten everything I wanted out of the bargain. I've experienced a good relationship, though a fake one. It's shown me what I really should be looking for, not what I have to settle for.

I'll stay the course, for Weston. Plus, who doesn't love a good party, right? And Wes's family? They do throw a hell of a party. I throw my last pair of clean leggings into the bag, knowing I'll end up in them sooner rather than later. I'm in my travel sweatpants since we're packed up fully and loading all of our belongings for the 11-plus hour drive. I'm glad we're used to being in the car together for long stretches of time, or this would be awkward. I've never road-tripped with a boyfriend before, but I've been on the road plenty with Weston and we're perfect car companions. I worked off this morning from my last shift and there's not an event until tomorrow night for the wedding so we have time to get there. Weston finished up his contract two days ago and has been helping me get all of my crap together.

When we planned all of this out, the wedding date being after our contract ended and the road trip to So-Cal and everything, we weren't together like we are now. I thought I would have found another contract by now. I thought we would be easier to move on from after the wedding. I thought there was no way I was going to fall for Weston. But here we are. No future plans other than the crazy dream of staying with Wes wherever he goes. I have never been *that girl.* I have never wanted to follow a guy around, never let someone else determine my future. Weston is just so different. I think he cares about me just as much as I do for him.

As soon as this wedding is over, we're going to have to talk. I can't continue to be too scared to ask for more. I want more. I know that now. But it terrifies the hell out of me.

It scares me even more to think about a future without Weston in it, though. And that's what I have to focus on if I want to find the courage to broach that topic.

I exhale, letting my eyes fall closed as I lay my hands atop my packed bag. I think through my checklist one more time before zipping the last compartment closed and looking around. I check under the bed and in every drawer one last time and come up empty. I don't think we're leaving anything behind. Except a whole lot of memories. This was our first place together, whether we were calling it that or not. My room was basically used as a closet for most of our stay here and my pillow lived in Weston's room.

I wander into the kitchen, pulling my luggage behind me and let the memories of this place wash over me. I see all of the sweet notes written out beside the coffee pot when I woke up for work. I feel the plushness of the couch pillows under my back as we watched copious amounts of reality TV. I hear Weston's laughter and smack talk as we played card games at the table. Games that would quickly turn into "loser strips." I smile, feeling so much gratitude to this place that was so transitory, yet so transforming.

"What's that smile for, beautiful? Thinking of me?" Weston says from behind me, taking the step to wrap me into his arms.

I laugh and say, "Just thinking of all of the great memories we've shared here. It's not usually this hard to leave a place."

"I know what you mean," Wes says, pressing his cheek into my hair. His words are a little muffled when he says, "This place was the beginning of something wonderful and it feels a little like we're leaving that behind somehow."

I feel tears forming, but I don't allow them to fall. Instead, I focus on the pressure of Weston's face against my ear. I focus on the feel of his thumbs grazing over my arms and his warmth against my back. I concentrate on the realness of this moment, not my fear of the future.

"Well," I say, once I feel the tears receding, "you packed up and ready to go?"

"Yes ma'am! You ready? You know I've been looking forward to the road trip snacks for a week now!"

I let Weston's excitement wash over me, cleansing away any last bit of sorrow.

I turn in his arms, letting him see the smile stretching my lips. It's as real as I can manage right now and I'm just hoping that it's enough. He reads my features for a moment, obviously noting that something is wrong. Thankfully, though, he doesn't push it. He lets me keep whatever is happening to myself, though I know he can read me like an open book.

Weston holds my gaze, dipping his face to mine. He presses the sweetest kiss to my lips, pulling me even closer to his chest. I don't want to leave this moment. Our bubble is due to pop and I'm nowhere near ready.

➤

We're four hours into our drive when I wake up from my nap. It's amazing how quickly I fall asleep in the car. Especially when Weston is driving. I feel safe and secure and it lulls me right to sleep. I stretch in my seat, sitting the back up so that I'm no longer laying.

"Well hey there sleepyhead. How are you feeling?" Weston asks, reaching over to run a knuckle across my cheek. The fact that he can do that without even looking means that he just knows where my cheek is going to be. I feel like that should unsettle me, but it's oddly comforting.

"I feel much better. A little catnap is just what the doctor ordered," I reply. I rub my eyes a little, trying to clear the fog.

"Four hours counts as a 'little catnap?'"

"Of course! Have you seen how much cats sleep?" I ask, laughing louder than I intended.

Weston's smile stretches across his face, lighting his eyes. "I love when you laugh like that. It sounds a little out of control. It's perfect."

I feel heat steal across my cheekbones, warming through to my heart. I can't let his use of the "L-word" affect me like this. It was just something off-handed. He's not telling me that he loves *me*, just something *about me.*

I thrust my hand over into Weston's space, grasp his hand and hold on tight. If we're going to be fake dating through the weekend, I'm going to take full advantage. Any touch is almost enough.

"Afraid I'm going to make you drive at the next stop, little passenger princess?" Weston asks, bringing my hand up to his lips for a quick kiss.

"No, you wouldn't dare. I just like touching you sometimes. It reminds me that you're real," I say, trying not to care about how vulnerable that sounded.

A weird look comes across Weston's face but he quickly pulls it into a smile. Instead of responding verbally, however, he just pulls my hand back to his lips. He places a gentle kiss to each fingertip, showing me that he feels the same way.

I clear my throat, unwilling to let him see how much just that small touch of his mouth makes me want to park this car and get him undressed.

"So, um, when is our next stop anyway?" I ask.

Weston looks over to his phone on the dash, scans the GPS pulled up and says, "Probably about 30 minutes. Can you make it that long?" He spares me a small glance, winking at me with that smartass smirk.

"Yes, buddy. I can make it a half hour. I haven't been awake long enough to have drank anything and I peed before we left. Thank you very much." I roll my eyes, knowing that will earn some sort of response.

I'm rewarded with a growl before Weston says, "Roll your

eyes at me again and I'm make them roll myself."

Jesus. Maybe I can't make it 30 minutes. I shift in my seat, trying to get some much-needed friction. This only serves to pull a dark chuckle from Weston's chest.

"Okay, if you're going to be saying things like that, we might need to stop before that half hour mark." My skin is still burning and I'm on the verge of rolling my window down.

"I mean, I just saw a sign for a rest station about a mile up the road. You need me to stop there? Help you...stretch out? It has been a pretty long ride so far. I could do with getting some blood pumping." Weston is sporting the biggest, shit-eating grin right now and I can't help but smile in return.

"Not if you're going to be using innuendos like that. I think I've cooled right back off, but thanks," I reply, not trying to hide my smirk.

"Alright, we'll just stick with the original plan then. Half an hour to the next stop. Then maybe some sex."

"Oh my God, shut up!" I cry, smacking his arm with my free hand.

We both dissolve into giggles, not quieting until we're at the gas station.

Chapter 43

Weston

I don't think I've ever had so much fun in the car before today. We've always been great travel companions, but the energy in the vehicle on the way to So-Cal was amazing. There was so much laughter and many inappropriate jokes.

We roll into our hotel for the weekend around 8 p.m. and immediately head to the room. We drop our bags, freshen up and head right back downstairs. We have tonight together and tomorrow starts the big party. Tomorrow night we'll have a big meet and greet at a local brewery for all of the out-of-town guests. Friday is the rehearsal dinner and the wedding is Saturday night. I'm not a groomsman, but I have to be there early for pictures and of course to walk my sister.

I can't believe this week is finally here. I'm so excited to get to watch my sweet sister get married. And I can't wait to party it up at the reception. If this wedding is like any of the others that my family has thrown, it will be fun. And Kiera, even though she's the sweetest of us, can get down with the worst of us.

Grace and I find seats at the bar, ready to have a good meal and a stiff drink. I'm hoping to get some sleep before all of this wedding craziness kicks off.

"I'm really craving a steak. And some mashed potatoes. But this menu looks a little more like rabbit food," Grace says, her lips pulled to the side in concentration.

"Well, they have a plant burger," I say, pointing at the item on the menu.

"Yeah, not really the same. Hmm, they have street tacos. Those are probably good." A little line has appeared between Grace's eyes and it takes everything in me not to try to rub it away with my thumb.

"And sweet potato crisps. It's a type of potato...," I joke.

"You're right. I could do that. Street tacos and sweet potato crisps it is. What are you getting to drink?"

"Hmm....something spicy. They have several drinks with Tajin rims and I'm in the mood for *hot*."

Grace shakes her head, turning in her seat to look at me. "You just don't quit, do you?"

"Quit what? Being handsome and positively suave? No, I don't," I reply with my best imitation of a smolder.

Grace just continues her head shake of derision, obviously not charmed by me. I'll have to try harder next time.

"So," I sigh, "are you ready for all of this? I know we've been leading here, but it's different when it's just the two of us. I feel like I'm putting an unfair amount of pressure on you."

"Weston, I'm a big girl. I can handle this. This is just an extension of what we've already made together. If we can fake this much for ourselves, I'm sure your family will have no problem believing we're together. Hell, even I forget sometimes," Grace says, dropping my eye contact on the last part and not looking back up.

"Grace," I start, but she just shakes her head, not allowing me to say what I want so desperately to say. It's not the right time and I know that. I'll have to wait.

The bartender chooses this moment to come take our orders, interrupting any chance we had to actually talk.

"I'll have the cucumber mojito," Grace tells the bartender.

I order my margarita with Tajin and then order some jalapeno poppers for an appetizer. Grace's head whips toward me before she says, "Hot, huh? You weren't kidding."

Our drinks are out quickly and we're sipping and stealing glances at each other. There have been so many moments in this not-very-fake relationship that should have been awkward and they just aren't. Everything feels so natural with Grace, it's hard to feel anything but.

We get our food ordered and when the poppers are in front of us, we dig in. We settle into our comfortable silence, snacking and sipping. We people watch, taking in our surroundings and savoring the fact that no one is talking to us like they will be the rest of the weekend.

I don't know if there's any way to be prepared for the amount of questions we'll be facing the next three days from every family member I've ever met and the ones I've only heard about. We've decided to just stick to the truth. We met in nursing school, were traveling together for work and hit it off. That's the simple version and pretty much what happened. Obviously no one needs to know that we hit it off on purpose, for the sake of a wedding date.

Grace and I have also decided to just play it as natural as possible. Touch when we want, but don't feel like we have to put on a PDA tutorial. Though, how I'll manage to keep my hands off of her at all remains to be determined.

I'm deep into my thoughts—mostly about how tonight could end—when I notice Grace turned fully around in her chair and staring.

I move to ask her what she's doing when she squeals and leaps from the bar stool. She takes off running across the bar before I can even get my stool turned.

"OHMYGOD ANSLEY!" Grace all but shrieks, rushing towards our friend.

I finally get my stool turned around and make my way across the floor as well. Much slower than Grace made her trip, however. I watch as the women embrace, pulling each other into the fiercest hug I've ever seen.

"Ugh I've missed you so much," Grace says into Ansley's shoulder.

"Same girl. We haven't gotten a chance to even video chat since the trip and I have missed this beautiful face," Ansley replies, her hand sliding up to Grace's cheek. Grace leans into the touch and I can see the tears welling up in her eyes. I didn't realize she hasn't been able to talk to our friends as much recently. I'm sure their schedules have just been weird.

I make it to the edge of the women's orbit when Ansley looks up and meets my eyes. "Well hello, Weston. Just the man I came to see."

Chapter 44

Weston

"Huh?" I say, my mouth hanging open like a dead fish.

"I'm sorry, what now?" Grace says, ever the more eloquent of us.

"I'm so excited to see you, Grace. And we are going to catch up. As soon as I talk to Wes here." Ansley gives me a very pointed look that has me a bit terrified.

Okay, well this is weird. "Um, we were just finishing up dinner. I'm not sure what to do here…," I say, glancing at Grace. Her face shows just as much confusion as I'm feeling. At least we're together on that.

"I'll just go ahead and head up to the room. I need to get some stuff unpacked and hung up for the weekend. You two talk and then I'll come back down or you can come up when you're done." Grace looks nervous, but I'm not sure why. Maybe she's just reading my anxiety.

"Okay love, we'll see you in just a minute. Get those pretty dresses hung up so they don't wrinkle," Ansley says with a smile towards Grace. Once Grace is around the corner, Ansley turns back to me with a look of extreme irritation on her face. "What the actual hell, Weston?!" she explodes in a whisper yell.

"What?" I asked, genuinely shocked at this turn of events.

"What the hell do you think you're doing? *Fake dating* Grace?! You know she has trust issues and you're going to start something with her without even making it real? I can't believe you! This is the most absurd idea you have ever had. How did you even get her to agree to this? And don't think I haven't been watching you since you walked in. Lexa filled me in on all of the details and I asked around about the wedding plans. You are even acting like a couple when you're not around your family. What is that about?" Ansley rambles through her dissection of what she has deemed the worst decision of my life. And I let her. She's not saying anything that I haven't thought of myself.

"Are you done?" I ask, once she strings two breaths together.

"For now. What do you have to say for yourself?"

"I love her."

Well, that's out there now.

It's Ansley's turn to gape at me, speechless since she began her tirade.

"Does she know that?" Ansley finally asks, voice quieter than a mouse.

"Not yet. I didn't want to talk to her about this when she's somehow under the impression that all of this is still us 'faking it.'" I say, shrugging. "I thought that if I waited until after the wedding, she would see that I really meant it. I don't want her to feel like I'm just trying to make the act more real for my family."

Ansley releases a large sigh and deflates some. Obviously her anger over this perceived wrongdoing on my part was the only thing keeping her upright. From the bags under her eyes and the state of her usually well-kept hair, I'd say she flew here right after work—with at least one layover.

"Don't tell me you flew out here by yourself? Where's Landon?" I ask, looking around for the first time.

Ansley looks sheepish as she admits, "Well he had to work and he also maybe thought I was being a little dramatic with the in-person surprise visit instead of just calling. But I was afraid you wouldn't listen or that I wouldn't be able to reach you. I had no idea this was what was really going on. From how Lexa described it, you and Grace were just friends with benefits. And I guess from the way Grace talks, she thinks she likes you more than you like her. Which in retrospect, I could have talked to her over the phone about as well. But that's not the point. I needed to see for myself what was going on with you two. You love her, huh? Well same. Do I have to give you the whole 'hurt her and we'll hurt you' talk or are you pretty well versed in that one?"

"I think I get the gist. I'm scared enough of you and Lex as it is, I don't need a speech," I say with a laugh.

Ansley punches me in the shoulder with a muttered, "Asshole."

"So, I'm assuming in the great haste to foil my evil plans, you didn't book a room right?" I ask, arching a brow at the brunette.

"Well, er, no. But I'm sure there's something nearby."

"No ma'am. You are our friend and you'll stay with us tonight. We have a pull out couch and I'll take that. You can sleep with Grace tonight. She'll probably be glad to get a night away from me."

"Okay, ew. But also, I can't ask that of you. You have plans tomorrow, you need to get sleep."

"Ans, I didn't offer to keep a midnight vigil. I offered a place to sleep for the night. I might get more sleep this way anyway."

"Again, ew," Ansley says with a fake gag.

"Alright, well while you decide your sleeping arrangements for the night, I'm going to go pay my tab. Be right back."

As I walk back to the bar, I hear, "Hey Lex...Yeah I talked to him. I'll have to text you all the details, but our boy is in love... .Yes, with Grace....No, we didn't get that far...Yes, I promise I didn't hit him." I laugh to myself as I leave eavesdropping range. This is not how I expected tonight to end, but the biggest thought running through my mind? I'm glad Grace has such amazing friends.

Chapter 45

Grace

"Sleepover?!" I scream as Ansley bursts through the door, flinging herself onto my bed.

"Sleepover!" she shouts, falling into my outstretched arms. We're a tangled mess of arms and giggles when I hear, "Oh boy, should've known this would be a bad idea." Weston is standing at the door, his impressive biceps bulging as his arms cross against his chest. If he wasn't smiling from ear to ear, I would have less trouble believing him.

"Mhm. You're just upset you lost your sleeping spot for the night," I say, sticking my tongue out at him. He returns the gesture but doesn't argue.

"Yeah, don't get him started. I heard all about how active you two are when you're sharing a bed. I don't need more of that imagery in my head," Ansley says, offering a grimace.

"You told her what?!" I screech, my attention turning back to Weston.

"Nothing. She just surmised based on a few choice phrases," Wes replies with a shrug.

I can't help but roll my eyes at this man, and when I look at Ansley she's doing the same. This causes a whole new round of giggles.

"So, is anyone going to tell me what the big talk downstairs was about?" I ask as soon as we quiet down.

"It was a misunderstanding. And not that I would normally admit this, but I'm glad it was. I was wrong and that's all. Discussion over," Ansley says in her matter-of-fact charge nurse voice.

"Yes ma'am," I say, giving her arm a little shove.

Weston opens his mouth to say something, a very serious expression on his face, but he's interrupted by the ringing of my phone. I glance down and see that the display shows my *abuela's* name. My face splits into a grin and I jump up from the bed, running to the bathroom.

"Isn't it like the middle of the night over there?" I hear Ansley ask.

Weston responds, "Uh, I think like 7 a.m.?"

It's actually 8 a.m. in Spain, but he was close enough. I close the door behind me and answer, "*Hola, abuela.* How are you?"

"Oh, Grace. I am wonderful. How are you doing? I know it's late over there. I just woke up this morning and wanted to hear your beautiful voice, *mi tesoro.*" My grandmother hasn't called me treasure in so long. I wonder if something has happened to make her feel nostalgic this morning.

"I'm well, *abuela.* Thank you for calling me. I'm glad to hear your voice as well. What plans do you have for the day?" I ask, wanting to keep her on the phone.

"Your *abuelo* and I are going to the market this morning. I'm wanting to cook him a new dish tonight and we need a few ingredients," she replies.

"That sounds like a wonderful day. How is *abuelo*?" I ask.

"He is very well. And while we are on the subject, any new man in your life? Someone for you to cook for?" Her tone is light, but I know she's serious. This is the question she always asks me.

"Actually, yes. I'm in Santa Clarita, California for a wedding this weekend as a man's date. He's really nice and I think that you would approve. He's gotten me to start drawing again." I blush with the last part of my sentence, thinking of the last drawing I completed. I haven't been able to look at anything else long enough to even attempt a new sketch. Talk about obsessed.

"That's wonderful, *mi tesoro*! I knew that art would pay off. I always told your *abuelo* that your art is how you would find a man."

What? I must have heard her wrong, I think. "I'm sorry *abuela*, I don't think I understood that last part. You meant that the right man would support my art, right?"

"No *tesoro*, we knew that your art would bring you the man. That's why we encouraged your drawing so much as a child. Now you can quit that job you've been having to work and start raising babies. And you can keep your art as a nice little hobby," she says whimsically, like she's not shattering my entire view of my childhood. I always thought they wanted me to draw as a way to make a living for myself, express my creativity or hell, just because I liked it. I never imagined my family wanted me to draw as a way to "find a man." How does that even work?

I'm so speechless that *abuela* thinks I've hung up. "Grace, Grace, are you still there?"

"Yes, *abuela*, I'm here. Sorry, I just...was shocked, I guess. I always thought you wanted me to draw because I was good at it and you were proud."

"Oh, *tesoro*, of course I'm proud of you. I'm always proud of you. But *mi cariña*, it is no way to support yourself. It's how you set yourself apart to find someone to support you."

I'm near tears, realizing that my childhood trips to the museums, all of the art supplies and every conversation we had about art all revolved around me securing a relationship for a man to financially support me. This is not how I was raised, not by my parents and definitely not by my Grammy. I'm sure she is rolling over in her grave listening to this conversation.

"Um, *abuela*," I say, knowing that I can't continue to talk to her about this, "I gotta go. It's pretty late here and we have an early day tomorrow." I pull my phone from my face, sniffling and trying to dry my tears before they fall. "Goodnight, and we will talk soon. *Te amo, abuela.*"

"Of course, *mi tesoro.* Have sweet dreams and we will talk again very soon," she says, so sweetly.

I knew that my family is Spain was much more traditionally minded than my American grandparents, but I guess I never realized the extent. My *abuela* talking about finding a man to support me and not needing to work a job anymore and cooking for my husband was too much for me. Obviously, I want to cook for Weston—I want him to try my family dishes. Er, uh, whoever I'm with.

I sit on the edge of the tub, phone in hand, and stare at my reflection in the mirror. I view myself differently than how my family does, most certainly. But who has the right view? I am Grace, a nurse and an artist. I help people and I see the beauty in things. That's who I am, regardless of how I got my start in life. The way my family sees me does not determine my self-worth and will not change my self-confidence. I am me.

I steel my nerve, knowing that I can't go back out into the room looking like I've been crying. Weston and Ansley will ask me a thousand questions and I am not ready to talk about this.

With a final deep breath, I stand and square my shoulders. I give myself one more good look in the mirror, reminding myself who I am. I reach for the door handle and pull it open—and run right into Weston's chest.

"Why are you crying? Is everything okay? Did something happen?" Weston and Ansley pepper me with the questions I dread.

I can't help the tears that start sliding down my cheeks. I wipe them away as fast possible, but it's nowhere near quick enough. I see the twin looks of pity on the faces of my two closest friends and it breaks me down even further.

"Come here, buddy," Wes says, pulling me into a tight embrace. He cradles my face against his shoulder, letting me soak his shirt with my tears. I cry for longer than I want to, but eventually I dry up. I pull back, wanting to look in Weston's eyes, needing him to see that I'm okay. I feel my lower lip quivering, but I keep the tears at bay by some miracle.

"Do you want to talk about it?" Ansley says from my side.

"Not really. But also yes?" I whimper.

"Here, let's go sit," she says, taking my elbow to gently lead me back to the bed.

The three of us sit on the edge of the bed with me sandwiched in the middle. I let out another little sniffle and Ansley takes my hand. Weston has the other clasped between his two large, warm palms.

One deep breath, then two. "So apparently, my grandparents only encouraged my art as a child because they thought it would help me find a husband to support me. When I told my grandmother that I was seeing someone, she immediately started gushing about how I could quit my job and all that crap. It was just a lot at once. Especially since I just finally started drawing again and now I don't know if I want to anymore and…"

"Shh, breathe Grace. Just breathe," Weston murmurs into my hair, running his hand down my back in a soothing motion.

"Of course you'll still draw. You love it and like you said, you just got your love for art back. You draw and say to hell with the stereotypes your family are trying to force on you," Ansley says, giving my hand a squeeze.

There's a long moment of silence in which I just sit and let my friends comfort me. I let out a few more sniffles, but the crying is done for now.

"So, um," Weston starts, "I know this is obviously not the important part of your story, but you told your grandmother you were dating someone?"

Ansley reaches behind my back and slaps Weston's arm. "So not the time!" she says, but I can tell she's on the verge of laughter.

I start giggling, leading Ans and then Weston to join in. We fall back on the bed with me still snuggled in between. I sigh loudly, letting out all of my feelings.

"You gonna be okay?" Ansley asks, reaching over to pat my hand.

"Yeah, I am. I guess I was kinda shocked. And my emotions feel a little heightened right now. I'll be fine. My family doesn't dictate my self-image. At least that's what I told myself in the mirror before I came out of the bathroom, anyway," I chuckle.

I don't think that I was prepared to be this open with my

thoughts tonight but here we are. I think it's being at this high-stakes wedding that's really getting to me. Knowing that we will be going out there tomorrow and putting on a performance for his family has me wanting to put mine and Weston's relationship into a neat little box. We act like one thing and say we're another, I barely know how to tell what's real anymore.

Weston and Ansley snuggle into me on either side and I can only hope it's enough to hold me together through the weekend.

Chapter 46

Weston

What the hell is wrong with Grace's family? Why would her grandmother tell her that her art was only worth the man it would bring into her life? That's not how this works.

I mean, really. She still drew in college, but she had long since stopped by the time we were hanging out and if that's what her grandmother thinks was my main point of attraction, she's very wrong. Now that I know what talent she has, it seems crazy to me that she spent so much time not pursuing her passion.

As amazing of a nurse as she is, I know it's not something she's going to spend her life loving. Bedside nursing is a hard career and I'm so proud of the energy and love she pours out for her patients. I couldn't do it. If I could help cultivate an opportunity for her art to thrive, I would jump on it. And I would never, ever tell her that she's not good enough to earn a living.

I can't get these thoughts out of my head as I lay on the pullout couch in our hotel room. Grace and Ansley fell asleep hours ago. I can tell by Grace's soft snores. I'm glad she's getting some good sleep after her emotional roller coaster of a day. I can't imagine having my family say something like that to me.

Though, I am the one bringing a fake date to a family wedding just because I don't feel that I can tell them the truth of our relationship. Of course my mother would understand fully. But I'm not willing to spill my guts about this woman in front of her and all of my sisters when I know I'm already going to be emotional about Kiera.

I toss and turn for another half hour until I hear a hiss from the bed and a quiet, "If you don't be still, I'm going to come over there and knock you out." I stop immediately, knowing Ansley well enough to take her threats seriously.

Within minutes, my mind has finally stopped churning long enough for me to drift off. We have a long weekend ahead of us and I need some sleep.

➤

I had planned for breakfast in bed this morning. A good start to our last day in our bubble, before the brewery tonight. But that is squashed when I wake up to Ansley and Grace staring at me from the bed.

"Can I help you ladies?" I ask, rubbing the last of the sleep from my eyes.

"We're very hungry and we wanted to go downstairs and eat. But we didn't want to wake you so we were just sitting here, waiting," Grace says, faking a look of innocence.

"Mhm. Well let me just tell you. It's creepy as hell to wake up to you two staring at me all round-eyed like that," I mutter.

"Okay well sorry. But...breakfast?" Ansley asks, less innocent than Grace by far.

"Yes ma'am. Do you two mind if I stop by the restroom first, or will you starve to death before I can empty my bladder?"

I get identical eye rolls for that comment, but I just laugh as I make my way out from under the covers and to the bathroom. I splash some water onto my face, making sure that I'm fully awake for this meal. I wish I could take a quick shower, but the girls might kill me and this hotel has probably seen worse than my greasy hair.

I run a brush through it anyway, trying to at least tame the curls at the top. I sigh, knowing I'm fighting a losing battle. After a quick scrub of the teeth, a flash of a smile to myself, I throw the door open.

"So, you're ready? Cool, let's go!" Ansley says, grabbing Grace's hand and waving for me to follow.

"Again, creepy. You can't just sit around and watch me and wait for me to be ready. You two can't like watch TV or play on your phones? Like normal people?" I scoff, hand gesticulating in the air wildly.

"Okay drama king, let's go. I'm starving," Grace says. I follow them out of the hotel room and to the elevator banks. I watch as the numbers rise to our floor and listen to the girls talk about the most mundane things I could never imagine even thinking. How do their minds keep this much information sorted?

It's honestly astonishing. I shake my head, trying to clear it of these thoughts. It's too early for this. I'm used to getting up early for work, but my brain feels fuzzy this morning. I must not have slept very well on that pull-out couch last night.

By the time we make it downstairs, I finally feel my hunger creeping in. My stomach growls loudly as we exit the elevator and Grace turns around with a side-eye glare towards me. "So you are hungry, huh? Mr. I'm-gonna-sleep-all-morning."

"It is 7 a.m., not the middle of the morning. I would be in a less grumpy mood if I would've had a better sleeping partner than that crusty couch mattress," I reply with a side-eye of my own toward Ansley.

Ansley throws her hands up in a gesture of "whatcha gonna do about it?" and smiles.

The smells from this breakfast place entice my stomach to rumble even louder.

After an eventful breakfast, Grace and I say our goodbyes to Ansley. "I'll let you two have some privacy, I'll be over here," I say, hooking a thumb towards the elevator bank.

I watch as Grace pulls Ansley into a tight hug, both of them laughing. I can overhear some of their conversation, knowing that they aren't trying very hard to be quiet.

"I'm just a phone call away," Ans says. She cuts her eyes to me, trying to remind me she's talking to me as well. I smile and nod slightly, letting her know I hear her loud and clear.

"Yes ma'am, you know I'm always here for you, too. And thank you for coming all the way out here just to check on me. I can't even begin to tell you how much it means to me," Grace replies, pressing a kiss into Ansley's cheek.

I smile again, watching the sweetness of this moment and thanking our lucky stars once again for our amazing friends.

Chapter 47

Grace

What a whirlwind of emotions this weekend has been, and we haven't even had the ceremony yet. I know I'm a crier at weddings so there's hardly any point in putting anything but waterproof mascara on for the rest of the trip.

I still can't quite wrap my head around the conversation with my *abuela* last night. I guess looking back on it, I should have had an inkling of their mindset. My mom told me that when she and my dad got married, my grandmother had lots of "words of wisdom" to hand over. *Abuela* apparently flat out told my mother that it would be inappropriate for her to be working outside of the home when they started having children. Knowing that they wanted kids, but that she also wanted a career and an income of her own, my mom promptly ignored this "advice." There's always been some contention over the fact. Maybe I just assumed there were different rules for grandkids than kids and since I wasn't marrying her son, *abuela* wouldn't try to impose the same restrictions.

I have too much of my mom in me to abide by traditions that

I feel to be so outdated. I can't imagine not working for my own way in life and I love having a career in a field I'm passionate about. I tend to count myself lucky in that regard.

It's been a few hours since Ansley left after breakfast and we've decided a lazy day in bed is just what the doctor ordered. Weston has me tucked into his side, my leg thrown over his and we're snuggled under the plush duvet. Some nonsense reality show is playing on the TV and I'm so thankful for this time with him.

"This is nice," I say, tipping my head back to be able to meet Weston's eyes.

A sweet smile overtakes his mouth and his bends to place a soft kiss to the tip of my nose. "It is. I could cuddle with you all day, buddy." As if the prove his point, he pulls me further into him, causing my hand to slide from his chest to his side. I give him a tight squeeze of a hug and I'm rewarded with the rumble of a chuckle against my cheek. I can hear the steady drumming of his heartbeat and it's one of the most soothing sounds I could ever imagine. I'm close to dropping into a nap when I hear, "You know you're amazing, right? Smart and driven and talented and compassionate and..."

I peel myself off of Weston's chest to place a kiss to his mouth. I'm overcome with emotion, but I also need him to stop. I'm too close to crying again.

"You're not so bad yourself, buddy," I say, trying to lighten the mood a bit.

It doesn't seem to work though, because the earnestness on Weston's face doesn't go away and there's a gleam in his eye that warns me of words I'm not ready to hear from him yet.

Even though I know I'm in love with this man, I cannot hear it from his mouth right now. There's too much going on in my head and this weekend means too much to him and his family for me to act like a crazy person.

"Grace, look at me," Wes says, using his finger to tilt my face toward his. "You know I mean it. I don't want you to ever doubt for one second how I see you or how I feel about you."

My breath stutters for a moment before I'm able to let in a full inhale. I smile, though it feels a bit wobbly. I really, *really* can't hear him finish this speech right now.

So instead of letting him tell me, I decide to show him how I feel. I take his face in my hands, holding it like the precious thing it is and I place a gentle, salty kiss on his full mouth. I didn't realize that I had started crying, but the silent tears are falling now, running over my chin. Weston uses his thumbs to wipe the tears away before letting his fingers slide into my hair. He kisses me back like he knows what I'm trying to convey. I can only hope that he knows that I feel the same way for him.

We tangle ourselves further into the sheets, letting our bodies do the work our minds can't.

I'm a panting mess, being held together by Weston's strong hands. Sweat slicks our bodies, but when I look into Weston's eyes, the love shining there is what undoes me completely.

➤➤

The afternoon passes in that same lazy haze, both of us willing to ignore the words our mouths were trying to form. I have never felt this way before. I thought I was in love with my ex that I dated through college. But the second our five-year plan didn't add up, I was like *it's been nice knowing ya!* I can't imagine feeling that way about Weston. If he told me tonight that he wanted to move to Antarctica and become a penguin researcher, I'd be there. I'd complain about the cold the entire time, but I know we'd find ways to keep warm.

I'd follow this man anywhere. And that scares the absolute hell out of me.

My thoughts are interrupted by Weston turning toward me, an expectant look on his face.

"Yes, Mr. Anders?" I ask, failing to contain the smile creeping onto my lips.

Weston smiles back, and it's just as breathtaking as the first time he trained it on me. "I was just gonna say, it's probably time to be getting ready. We have to be at the brewery in an hour. You ready to get moving?"

I let out an entirely too dramatic sigh, my body going limp with resignation. "Ugh, I guess," I say with a smirk.

"Brat. I'll throw you in the shower and dress you myself if you don't get up." Weston lunges forward, making to scoop me up into his arms. I squeal and scramble out from under the covers. "Yeah, that's what I thought," he scoffs.

"Keep that up and see if I let you have any warm water," I say, strutting toward the bathroom, throwing my hair up into a messy bun on the way.

"You act like I'm not going to be in there with you, buddy," Wes says, lifting me off the ground and over his shoulder with way too much ease. I smack his butt with fervor, earning a deep chuckle but not my release.

"That water better be scalding by the time you put me under the spray, or I might smother you in your sleep tonight," I say, no real heat to the threat.

"You wouldn't dare. At least wait until Sunday. Wouldn't want to mess up the sister's wedding weekend with my murder and all."

"Oh you're right. How considerate." I stroke my chin between my thumb and forefinger like a bad movie villain, still plotting Weston's demise. Lucky for him, the point is moot once I'm under the water. It's the seventh circle of Hell hot, just like I like it.

I somehow manage to keep my hands to myself, just going through my shower routine. With the heated glances Weston keeps raking over my body, his mind is still in the same place as mine. If it wasn't an event for his sister's wedding, I'm almost positive we'd be back on that mattress.

Miracle of miracles we both make it out of the shower and back to the closet to get into our clothes. Weston shimmies his muscular thighs into his slacks, leaving them unbuttoned so he can tuck his shirt in a bit. But for now, I'm treated to his butt looking amazing in those pants paired with his very nice looking, naked upper body. He runs the towel over his hair once before throwing a knowing smirk in my direction.

"Oh, just go finish up in the bathroom so I can get in there for my makeup," I laugh. He's such a shameless flirt. And I love every minute of it.

My makeup routine is not too involved for tonight so it takes no time at all. Before I know it, we're both fully dressed and ready to mingle.

And all of a sudden, I feel like crying again. God, my emotions are all over the place. Just as the waterworks are springing up, Weston turns to me, places his palm against my cheek and says, "You look beautiful tonight and I'm proud to have you by my side this weekend. You're going to have to help me hold it together." And just like that, he's ignited my caretaker instincts, drying up my tears and making me smile brightly.

On arrival to the brewery, we're crushed into a frenzy of hugs and air kisses—even some real lips to cheek contact. Weston's entire family has come to California to make sure Kiera has an amazing weekend. Our blushing bride is in the center of the lounge area, seated on a plush velvet sofa and looking every bit the princess.

Of all of Weston's sisters, it's Kiera that I can most picture as a long-lost royal. She's all long lines, elegance and graceful movements. And I love everything about her. She's the life of the party and the person who will be the first to comfort you through a hard day.

The enchantress calls me to her sofa, patting the spot beside her, and how can I resist?

"Grace! I'm so glad you're here!" Kiera squeals. She wraps her arms around me, pulling my face close before she whispers, "And how is my baby brother treating you?"

I feel the blush steal over my cheeks and I sputter for a moment before landing on, "Perfectly, of course. But how are you, you gorgeous siren?"

Kiera laughs brightly, causing my smile to stretch open. "You little brat. I've been talking about me all night. But sure, I'll gladly do it some more." She winks a green-gold eye at me. "I'm splendid. Ready for this party to get started. I'm so excited for the reception. Oh and the nuptials, of course." She throws a sweet smile over her shoulder toward Nick. He just smiles back at her, ever indulgent.

"Of course the whole, ya know, getting married part," I laugh. "I'm excited to see your dress!"

"Wanna see a picture? I have one from every angle at this point!"

"No silly, I can't wait to see it on you. In person. That's the best part of the whole wedding!" I throw my hands up to frame my excitement, knowing she gets it.

A small, secretive smile steals over Kiera's face before she leans in to whisper, "So when do we get to go dress shopping for yours?"

My mind slams to a halt—wanting to ask what she could be talking about while also attempting to maintain the relationship ruse. What comes out of my mouth is, "Soon, maybe?"

A grin splits her face and I'm frozen in horror at the fact that I've basically just told Weston's sister that we're near an engagement. We aren't even *dating*. What is wrong with me?

I'm so trapped in my thoughts that it takes a moment to realize that I've been hauled off of the sofa and into male arms. Luckily the arms belong to my best friend and not some stranger. I would never make it in a scary movie. "You okay, buddy?" Weston says, mouth close to my ear while he wraps me in a hug.

"Huh? Oh yeah, sure. I'm fine. I just um...maybe...though accidentally...might have...," I stutter.

Wes leans down to peer into my eyes, his milk chocolate irises arresting my thoughts. "Spit it out. Did you step on Nick's foot or kill his mom's sister's friend's goldfish?"

I stumble over a chuckle before finally saying, "I just basically told your sister that I'm expecting a proposal in the near future and that I'd love to take her wedding dress shopping. And you know, seeing as how I don't have a *boyfriend*, finding a *fiance* that soon could be a problem." I can feel the heat rising from my chest into my face. My heart is beating far too fast and I may be a bit short of breath. It was one thing when I was imagining how tonight would go, it's something else actually living it.

"Well," Weston says, not letting go of my arms, "I can almost guarantee she's not expecting like some random dude to be the one proposing–she's probably assuming it's me.

So, that's one problem solved. And the other? I wouldn't worry about it too much. We'll have our time with family this weekend and then you don't ever have to talk to them again if that's what you would like. She's not going to be calling you up to go dress shopping if they no longer think we're together, right?"

Confusion wars with relief in my brain. Is this what he wants? This weekend of being together for show and then we'll just call it quits? I mean, I know that was the original plan, but that was months ago. I kind of thought that things between us had changed. Maybe I was wrong. Maybe I'm seeing things much differently than him.

I smile, trying to pull myself from the storm raging in my thoughts. "Yeah, of course. Just another ex that they'll happily ignore once the weekend is over." I feel Weston flinch against me, but he doesn't argue.

"Okay, well I think it's high time for one of these craft beers and some tapas. What d'ya say?" I shimmy out of Weston's embrace, giving him one more tight smile before turning on my heel and heading to the bar.

It feels like a kick to the gut—being reminded that though my feelings may be very real, this relationship is not.

I'm an artist, however, so I'll just have to continue to put on a show.

Chapter 48

Weston

What the hell was *that* about? Why was Grace all of a sudden freaking over a fake engagement and acting like we're not something else at this point. Granted, we haven't used the whole boyfriend/girlfriend label, but that's what we are right?

And why was my immediate defense mechanism to tell her it wouldn't matter because my family would never see her again? Of course they will! This relationship will be going long after this weekend. Hell, even if it does take a proposal to convince her that I'm serious about her, about *us*.

I follow her to the bar, knowing that it's time for major damage control. But, where to start?

"One Hazy Susan, please," Grace says to the bartender, offering that gorgeous smile that always makes me a little weak in the knees. She turns to me, eyebrow raised in question.

I step up to the bar and survey the options. "Oh, y'all serve beers from other breweries around the country as well?" I ask, noting a few familiar names.

"Yeah man, we like to import some new ones every few

months to give the locals more variety. We only brew about five different beers on site. See anything you'd want to try?" he asks, wiping his hands on a towel before slinging it over his shoulder in a classic bartender move.

"Does that one there say it's from Savannah, Georgia? I have friends living out there. Let me get that one," I finally decide.

"This one is a new favorite here. It's from PaCo Brewery in Savannah. A pilsner, so it's easy to drink. But people swear they can taste just the barest hint of orange peel in it, giving it a nice citrus aftertaste."

I give the beer a swig, letting it sit on my tongue before swallowing. I smile when the citrus makes my mouth tingle ever so slightly.

"That's delicious. I'll have to see if my friends have been to PaCo and maybe I'll hit it up next time I'm eastward."

The bartender gives me a gracious grin when I slip some cash into his tip jar after paying.

As we're walking toward the food, I glance over to see Grace trying—and failing—to hide a smile.

"What's that going on with your mouth? Got something sour in there?" I ask, knowing she's dying to talk.

"No, buddy," she says, rolling her eyes. "PaCo is where Drew works with Patrick and Connor. Pa...Co...? Drew is their head of marketing...? Didn't you find all of this out in St. Croix last year?"

"Oh right," I say. Why did that suddenly leave my brain? My mind must be other places tonight.

"Drew is getting promoted to chief marketing officer or something next month. Ansley told us that last night," she continues.

"Did she? I must have missed that part of the conversation,"

I muse.

"Well, to be fair, we might have actually talked about it in bed before you yelled at us for talking too much in the morning," Grace says, using her thumb to stroke her chin in a mock thinking pose.

"'Yell' feels like such a strong word for me asking you two to stop giggling like hyenas before I even had coffee."

"Tomat-oe, tomat-oh," she says, waving a hand flippantly.

I pull her into my side, leaning down to whisper, "You're such a brat," into her ear. She shivers slightly but doesn't pull away. I take full advantage of her closeness and press a kiss to the top of her head. She smiles down into the beer before taking a small sip. When she finally looks up at me, her nearly black eyes are so full of love and hope, but the small v between her eyebrows warns me of her worried thoughts.

"Hey, we probably need to talk some when we get back to the room tonight," I say, letting her pull away from me again. Why does the distance she's putting between us suddenly feel insurmountable?

"Yeah, absolutely," she says with a sigh. I move to pull her back to me but her attention is caught by my mom. She's making her way toward us, feral delight on her face. My mother looks radiant tonight, a light blue dress gracing her body. She moves toward us like a jungle cat on the prowl. I suddenly feel like a small prey item, stuck and staring into the face of danger. Of course, Grace and my mom have met when she's visited while we've been on assignment. But this is different. This is my mom meeting Grace as my *girlfriend*. My fake girlfriend, I struggle to remind myself yet again. She's already making her post-Weston life plans.

"Hey, you two! Don't you both just look wonderful," my

mother says, planting a kiss on both of our cheeks. I can see the radiance of Grace's smile from the corner of my eye and it's taking all of my willpower to focus on my mom instead of turning to bask in the glow.

"Hello, Rebecca," Grace says, stepping into my mother's outstretched arms. "You look lovely. That dress really brings out your eyes." Grace holds her at arm's length, doing a full review of the outfit. I see color creep into my mom's cheeks and know that Grace is charming the pants off of her right now. I feel the pain, she does that to me pretty much every day.

Mom turns fully toward me for the first time, stepping back to study me. I tower over her small frame. The girls and I all got our height from my father thankfully. Mom barely reaches Grace's shoulders. I let her look her fill, even gracing her with a full spin. "Oh my, my sweet boy. You look taller every time I see you. And even happier than I could have hoped," Mom says, giving Grace a wink with the last part.

I blush, daring to turn towards Grace, wanting to try to gauge her reaction. But, she's just smiling at me, eyelashes fluttering in a damn near perfect imitation of flattery and love.

I grimace slightly, but pull my lips up into a tight smile. There's no way she didn't take my offhand comments about my sister's nosiness as something awful. This is a very obvious act she's putting on. Though, I'm the only one here that knows her well enough to see that. I shake it off, trying to turn my thoughts towards something better, more appropriate for the current conversation.

"Well, Mom, who wouldn't be happy getting to share in his big sister's joy? You and Nick's parents have done an amazing job getting all of this planned. I love the family gathering before the rehearsal dinner. Those things are always a little stuffy, in my opinion."

Grace chuckles beside me, no doubt remembering the drama that occurred at the last rehearsal dinner we went to. I'm so thankful that Drew and Lexa and Jackson got their stuff figured out.

I've lost the thread of the conversation by the time I tune back in. Grace is talking about our latest hospital I believe, maybe our friends we met there.

"And you got to explore the area some?" Mom asks, knowing that's our favorite part of the road trip.

"Oh yes, we did. We took a little weekend trip to one of the neighboring cities and your son took me to the nicest restaurant. We spent a wonderful rainy day inside a lush hotel there. It was...," she stops abruptly, red staining her cheeks.

"It was a great day for Grace to work on her art, so that's what we did," I finish for her.

"Oh, that's lovely! I would love to see some of your drawings. Weston says you have quite the talent. What's your specialty?" Mom asks innocently.

I know where Grace's thoughts are, because mine are living in the same location. I groan a bit under my breath, trying to keep my mind in a safe place.

"Mostly pencils, but I've been experimenting with some charcoal recently as well." Grace's face is almost completely red at this point. And if I'm not mistaken, she's wriggling a bit. No doubt trying to contain the need to clench her thighs. I'm having just as tough of a time—my brain flashing back to the images of the day we shared in that hotel room, playing through my mind like a dirty movie.

My mother's eyes widen slightly, looking between us with a dawning realization on her face. She opens her mouth, but thankfully we're saved by the arrival of Carmen and her wife, Lisa. I whirl toward them, yanking them into a huge hug like the life raft they are.

"Yo, baby bro, you're crushing the air from my lungs," Carmen says, poking her fingers into my ribs to make me let them go. She knows how ticklish I am and she has always used it against me.

Lisa is smiling like a lunatic when I release them, immediately pushing past me to pull Grace into a hug. "I've heard so much about you from Car! I've been dying to meet you since the news spilled that you two were *finally* together." She takes a small breath before adding, "Also, you earned me a good fifty bucks. I was closest to the date."

Carmen smacks her arm, making her let go of Grace. Grace, whose mouth is hanging open like a fish. Grace, who is staring at me like a deer in headlights. I take that as my cue to ask, "I'm sorry what? You assholes had a betting pool on my dating life?"

Lisa's eyes widen into saucers as she takes a tentative step back. She shrugs and lets Carmen take the reins. "Well, we had a small bet regarding *when* you would start dating, or at least when you would tell us it was official. It was inevitable and we figured we could have some fun with it. It's not like we thought you would find out," she says, shooting daggers at Lisa's clearly apologetic face. Her hands fly up in defense as her mouth flattens into a line.

I laugh, trying to ease the guilt from Lisa's face. "It's honestly okay. It's not like it's super weird and embarrassing or something. Right, Grace? Such a totally normal thing for sisters to do," I say, raising an eyebrow in Carmen's direction.

"Well, considering my only child status, it's kinda hard to

tell. But I think it's funny," Grace says with a shrug and a huge smile on her face.

"Traitor," I mumble, pulling her to me. The moment our eyes meet, her smile slips and her breath stutters. Damn, all I want is to whisk this girl away from this crowd and show her how I feel about her. Instead, I settle for a quick kiss to her cheek, and whisper in her ear, "You ready to pay for that later?"

I feel the shiver run up her spine, but Grace doesn't outwardly acknowledge my threat.

Chapter 49

Grace

Of course I can't control the reaction my body has to Weston, but my mind immediately gives me the harsh reminder that even though we won't be together come Monday, we can still do the thing we're good at. I want to tease him back and make him blush, but I can't find the willingness to try right now. I'm too tired, emotionally.

Between my grandmother dropping her little bomb onto my self-confidence and Weston reminding me that we're on borrowed time, I don't think I can handle any other hard things today, or this week.

Instead of flirting back, I just say, "No, that's okay. I'll behave." I can tell that Weston caught the monotone way that I delivered that statement. His eyes are boring into the side of my head. I can't bring myself to even smile at him to ease the tension at this point. I...just can't. I feel like a void, lost in the dark and sucking away everyone else's happiness.

"Excuse me, I need to run to the ladies' room. I'll be back shortly," I say, letting my hand run down his arm. I can give physical touch—if nothing else, I can give him that.

A sigh escapes my lips, but I hustle off to the restroom. I don't lift my head to meet anyone's eyes as I pass, just keeping my gaze on my feet.

I'm nearing the restroom, a stride away from the door when a hand clasps around my forearm.

I turn, thinking I'll be face to face with Weston. However, the light brown eyes that catch mine belong to Carmen. "Hey, you okay?" she asks, concern flooding her gaze.

"Yeah, I'm totally fine. Just needed to run to the restroom real quick," I say, trying to force a smile onto my lips.

"Yeah...not buying it, sorry. Did we upset you with all that talk of betting and stuff? That was just us being stupid. We love our little brother, but we love messing with him even more. We didn't mean any harm by it and I would hate to have you upset with us. You seem sad. Or mad. It's hard to tell, honestly. But Weston is looking at you like a lost puppy right now and that makes me think something is definitely wrong." Sure enough when I look towards him, Weston has to pull his gaze away from us.

I shake my head again, trying once more to tell her I'm okay. Instead though, I start crying.

"Oh, shit," Carmen says, ushering me into the bathroom before anyone else can see. "Oh shit, I'm so sorry. Do you want me to get Wes or something?"

"It's not you," I say, hiccuping through a sob. "I promise it's not. I just had a really hard night last night and my feelings are all over the place right now. I'm not even really sure what I'm crying about. I think I just needed to let it out."

"I definitely get that. I am always down for a good cathartic cry. Need a tissue? A hug? Space?" she rambles.

"I'm good. I just need to splash some cold water on my face or something. Just give me a minute. I'll be fine, promise," I say, though the tears still streaming down my face threaten to undermine me.

Carmen gives me one last, lingering look before huffing out a sigh and saying, "Well, if you're sure...I'll give you a minute. But if I don't see you back out here in 10 minutes, I'm coming back in."

"Yes ma'am," I say, letting a real smile shine through the tears.

She gives me a shaky grin and turns to leave the bathroom.

"Wait!" I say, reaching out to touch her shoulder. She turns back to me, eyebrows raised in alarm. "I just wanted to say thank you. For following me in here and making sure I'm okay. You should be out there celebrating with your sister and you're in here watching me be a blubbering mess." To further illustrate my point, I hurriedly sniff the running snot back up and swipe a hand across my eyes.

Carmen gives me a sweet smile and says, "Hey, you're family, too. You know that right? No matter what happens with you and Wes, we've still got you."

"Oh," is all I can manage before the tears begin anew. With that, Carmen takes her leave and closes the bathroom door softly behind her.

I go into a stall, unwilling to cry by the sink in case someone else comes in.

And it's there, surrounded by toilet paper and formica walls, that I come to a decision.

I'll just have to fake it until I make it.

I pull myself from the stall, taking in my bedraggled appearance in the mirror. I must have been crying harder than

I thought. I use some water from the sink to un-smudge my eyeliner as much as possible and wet a paper towel to dab at the redness on my cheeks. I put a cold rag on the back of my neck and take some steadying breaths. I give myself the best pep talk I can manage before steeling my resolve and removing the towel from my neck. I straighten my shoulders, put on my smile and walk out of the bathroom, head held high.

I toss my hair over my shoulder in my "tough girl" imitation, immediately running into a wall.

Nope. Not a wall. Just a hard body. Weston is standing outside the bathroom, arms across his chest and an indecipherable look on his face. I want to call it concern but his aggravated posture throws me for a loop.

"God, I was about to come in there after you," Weston says, his arms dropping and shoulders drooping as he moves toward me.

"I'm fine, just needed a minute. Why aren't you out there with your family?" I ask, my arms snaking across my chest in a defensive gesture that he clocks instantly.

He stops his advance, eyebrows raising in confusion. "You're obviously upset and I came to check on you," he says softly, reaching out to touch my arm.

"You don't have to do that, we're in private. None of them can see us, it's not necessary." My voice sounds harsh to my own ears and I know he can feel the tension radiating off of my body.

He takes my shoulders in both of his hands, turning me to fully face him. "Grace, what the hell is going on? They've all been private moments until now. You should know that I'm not wanting to touch you for *their* benefit. Please just look at me," he says, trying to tilt my face up to meet his.

I'm nothing if not stubborn and I resolutely keep my gaze downcast.

He just sighs, releasing my chin. "Okay, well we can talk more about this later of course. Is there anything I can do for you right now? I just want you to be okay."

"I'll suck it up and your family will never see this. Just give me a minute. I'll meet you back out there." I finally meet his eyes, trying and failing to give him a smile. My lips quiver in the most dramatic way before I'm pulled into his arms.

"Grace, please. I don't know what's going on and I'm scared," Weston breathes into my hair.

"Me too," is all I can say.

Chapter 50

Weston

What the actual...? "What are you scared about? Please talk to me," I beg.

Grace continues to shake against me, making it obvious that she is not going to be okay any time soon. I gently push her backwards until we're back in the bathroom. I lock the door behind us and pick her up, setting her on the sink counter.

Now that she's eye-level with me, I grab her face in my hands and force her to meet my gaze.

"Talk to me. It's just us. It's just me."

Grace sniffles hard, not saying anything for longer than I can almost stand.

Finally, she opens her mouth to say something. I don't know what I'm expecting but, "I can't do this anymore" is not it.

"I'm sorry, what?" I say, genuinely not understanding her.

"I can't keep doing this. It's getting confusing and I'm not sure I can mentally or emotionally handle it anymore. I just need this to end. I'm so sorry." Grace is finally holding my eyes, but it's like she's speaking another language. There's no way she's saying this. I'm...in love with Grace. I can't lose her. Not now, not ever.

Why the hell can't I just tell her that?

My mouth opens to say it when she cuts me off with a finger to my lips.

She continues, "I'm not going to ask you to stage a breakup or something on the weekend of your sister's wedding. I'm just saying maybe I'll sleep on the couch in our room tonight and we can just kind of avoid anything that's not a public appearance. I just can't—I won't continue to act like we're together in private when we're not. I'm not going to lose you as a friend by doing all of this and I feel like that's where we're heading. I need some time to get my head on straight and I can't do that while sharing your bed. I think we've gotten enough 'practice' over the last month to sufficiently convince anyone that we're dating."

I'm utterly speechless, still unable to fully comprehend the meaning of her words. All I've really gotten is that she's done and she's leaving me and I'm not allowed to touch her anymore. She doesn't love me like I thought she might. We're never going to get a chance to be together.

She must take my silence for acceptance, because she pats my hand and jumps down from the counter. She turns to look at her face in the mirror, running her fingertips under her eyes and fixing any stray hairs. She turns back to me with a fake-ass smile on her face. One that she obviously believes will convince anyone out there, not realizing that I see right through it.

"Alright, let's get back out there. I'm glad we were able to have this chat. I thought you were probably on the same page so it's good that we talked it out. You want another drink from the bar?"

I just nod my head, rendered mute by this sudden turn of events.

"Same thing?" I just nod again and turn to open the door for the woman who just stomped my heart into a pulp under her heel.

⇒→

What the girls don't know won't hurt them, I guess. Now is definitely not the time to talk to Kiera, but I don't even know that I should try to talk to any of my sisters tonight. I want the focus to stay on Kiera, not on whatever insane shit is happening with Grace. I mumble my way through conversations, pasting on a smile and trying my hardest not to look at Grace. Every time I catch myself glancing her way, my brain attacks me, showing me all of our best moments together and making me realize that those times are over.

I know I'm not doing a stellar job of hiding my emotions, but I really didn't need Carmen hunting me down and telling me to stop moping around like someone kicked my puppy.

"What's going on with your face? Why do you look like that?" Tessa asked me before I could even hug her. She was late getting here, as usual.

"What are you talking about? This is just my face. Maybe it would have looked different an hour ago when the rest of us got here," I reply, trying to divert this conversation away from me.

She doesn't even try to take the bait, instead leveling me with a glare I remember quite well from childhood. It's a "mom glare" if I've ever seen one, and believe me, I've seen my fair share. Growing up with four older sisters is like having five mothers sometimes. They each had their own version of the now-tell-me-the-truth-son look that they would use on me–that is, when they weren't the ones helping me get into trouble in the first place.

Tessa was–and continues to be–the main cause of chaos in the family. She lives a very free-spirit kind of lifestyle, which suits her just fine. But it always leaves us somewhat in the dark about her plans for events and just general day-to-day life. We weren't fully aware of her itinerary for this trip until about an hour before we were supposed to be at the brewery.

Rather than detract from, it only adds to her charm. She always shows up and that's what really matters.

"You know, baby brother, I know your face. I've seen it–and you–go through many things. So, when I ask you why you are currently sporting your 'Dad accidentally popped my favorite birthday balloon' face, it's because I can tell that something is wrong. Now, do you want to talk about it right here or elsewhere? We can wander outside for a bit?" Tessa asks, letting me feel like I have some choice in this matter.

"Outside would be nice. I could use some fresh air. You've already said hey to Ki and Nick right?' I ask, making sure I'm not hogging our older sister.

"Yes, mom. I've already hugged her. Let's go before someone tries to steal you away from me." She grabs my arm, pulling me through the throng of people milling around the bar and towards the patio.

Once we're outside, under the twinkling Edison bulbs and out of earshot of others, Tessa says, "Is it that girl? Did she do something? I'll fight her."

I'm so shocked, I laugh–loudly. It takes a moment to catch my breath and attempt an answer. When I look back at Tessa's face, I can see how serious she is. Her love for me and the tenacity of her protective instinct is enough to sober me. "Um, my face is probably most likely due to the current situation with Grace, but it's not necessarily *because of* her," I state, trying not to lie and trying to save Grace from having to meet my crazy sister in the parking lot of this brewery.

"That felt very evasive, but I'll let it slide for now. We'll circle back. Do you want to tell me why it is that this girl that I've heard so much about and that my own sisters were sending me pictures of earlier tonight is not even within 50 feet of you? When I walked in, there was an entire building of people between the two of you. I thought this was like the real shit or whatever." The way that she finishes that sentence makes me realize that Tessa has never been in love. And that makes me more sad than my current hopeless relationship. I frown, trying to find the words to explain why I'm sad or why my face looks like this or why Grace doesn't love me. But nothing comes out of my mouth. Instead, a tear rolls down my face.

"Oh. Oh, no. Little Wessy, you love her huh? Did you tell her and she didn't reciprocate or what?" Tessa asks while reaching out to try to fold me into her embrace. I've been taller than my sisters since I turned 14 but that hasn't stopped them from pulling me into the tightest hugs I've ever experienced.

"No, I didn't tell her. I didn't get the chance. It's all supposed to be pretend, but my feelings aren't and I don't know that I can turn them off."

I feel her stiffen slightly at my words, realizing too late that I've exposed us without thinking.

"We did this to you. I'm so sorry. Every video call we asked about you two and we forced you to declare something that wasn't there. You wouldn't be going through this if it weren't for us. What can I do to help fix it?" she asks, standing on her toes to brush my hair from my forehead.

I lean into the touch, realizing that I should have just trusted my sisters with this all from the beginning.

"Just be here. That's all I need. And don't tell Kiera, please. The last thing I want is for her to be worrying about me when she's getting married. I'll get myself sorted, promise," I say with a sigh, bending down to scoop Tessa into a hug.

"Of course, baby bro. As long as you promise me one thing," she says, pulling back to look in my eyes.

"What's that?"

"Don't give up on Grace," Tessa says, pursing her lips once before exhaling a sigh.

Chapter 51

Weston

It truly is a testament to the strength of our familial bond that each of my sisters checks on me throughout the night. I know Tessa didn't snitch on me to any of them, but they can read my face better than anyone in the world. I've been keeping Grace within sight, but trying not to overcrowd her at the same time. But the complete turn from our PDA showing-selves to this is enough to have everyone confused. Luckily, Grace has been keeping my mom pretty much occupied, so she hasn't noticed the strangeness.

"What is happening?" Kiera asks, sidling up to me at the bar near the end of the night.

"Well, sis, this is a bar, where they typically serve alcoholic beverages. You come up to the nice gentleman, request a beverage and then exchange money for the service and product. What else can I help with?" I look down at her just in time to see the scowl of impatience completely transform my beautiful sister's face.

"Ugh, I knew there was a reason we didn't live together

anymore," she scoffs.

"Besides that fact that we're both over 30, you're getting married and I'm traveling every 3 months to a new place? Yeah, it must be my winning personality that has kept us apart," I say with a smirk.

"I wouldn't say that it's *not* a reason," she says with an over exaggerated eye roll. "But seriously, you okay? You seem different than when we first got here."

"Just tired, Ki. It's been a long week finishing up our last assignment and packing again. And I honestly have had a few too many beers. They just have such a great selection here and I'm always looking for a new favorite." I tip the drink in my hand towards her with mock cheer.

Kiera eyes me warily, trying to determine if I'm telling the truth. I keep my face as neutral as possible, letting her study my profile while I sip. She eventually sighs, letting it go. "As long as that's all it is. I would hate to have to beat someone up before the rehearsal dinner tomorrow," she says, letting her gaze wander over to Grace. I laugh, knowing that if anyone in our family really endorses violence, it's the sister standing by my side right now.

"That won't be necessary. But thank you for always being my knight in glittering armor," I laugh, pulling my big sister into a bear hug.

"Anything for you. Now, this party is almost over. Why don't you go scoop up your lady friend and head to the hotel. Tomorrow morning starts a lot more activity. Speaking of, don't forget you're going to the golf course with Nick and some of the guys. You brought your clubs?"

"Ki, considering I've never golfed in my life, I don't own clubs. But I'll rent some tomorrow. What are you girls going to be up to?" I completely forgot about golf tomorrow. Maybe I can find a place for Grace to hang out while we golf and we can meet up after.

"We're going to the spa. Massages, mud baths, manicures and pedicures. Oh, I meant to ask! Do you think Grace would want to join? One of my girls can't make it to town until tomorrow night just before rehearsal so we have an empty spot. We'd love to have her with us."

Kiera is beaming at me and I've never been so relieved that someone else is having bad luck. I feel guilty for a moment, but shake it off enough to say, "I'm sure she'd love that. I'll ask here while we're on our way back tonight and text you with her answer."

"Perfect!" Kiera gives me a sweet little side hug before running off to rejoin Nick and some of the bridal party.

I head over to where Grace has my mom doubled over in fits of laughter. There's no telling what she's saying to her. I can't help the smile that spreads across my face as I watch these two giggling together. It means so much to me that they get along this well. Now, if only I can convince Grace that this is indeed real and we can continue to have these moments forever.

With my mind finally made up in that regard—and Tessa's last statement running through my head—I step up next to Grace and pull her into my side. She relaxes into my hold instantly, before obviously realizing that she's trying to put distance between us for whatever reason. She tenses slightly but I smooth my thumb over her shoulder, telling her silently that I'm not letting go.

I let the two women finish their conversation, barely able to keep my mind in the present.

"So we'll see you in the morning? The spa will have a little breakfast setup. I'm so glad this hotel is so full-service," my mom says, basically ignoring my entrance.

"Yes, Rebecca! I'm so excited!" Grace says, squealing and clapping her hands in excitement.

"And, don't tell anyone I said this–I'll deny it if you do–but, I'm glad you're coming instead of Junie. She's our cousin and I love her dearly, but God is she a talker. I'd really like to relax tomorrow, you know?" I suck in a fake gasp for my mom's benefit, knowing she wants this to seem like a dramatic revelation for Grace, and not something that my mom has said for every other event we've all been together for. Mom looks at me, her lips pressed into a thin line, before scoffing a quick, "Oh, hush. I don't want to hear it. I'm glad you'll be out of our hair tomorrow, too."

I place my hand on my chest, giving my best look of indignation. My faux outrage does nothing to stifle my mother's giggles, only adding to them it seems.

"Well I'll let you two get on with your night. Are you going back to your hotel?" Mom asks, her voice turning high and squeaky at the end like she wants to ask something much more personal.

"Yes mother, we are going to the hotel. To sleep and get ready for a long weekend." I shake my head but can't stop the chuckle that bubbles up at my mom's behavior. She always wants to be in our business, but doesn't want to seem nosy. Not that her nosiness is a secret in our family. "You can grill Grace on exact details tomorrow while you have her captive." I laugh in earnest now, seeing their twin expressions of horror at my statement. My mom's is for outing her plans and Grace's is due to the realization that those plans will most definitely be coming to fruition tomorrow.

Still laughing, I drop my arm from Grace's shoulder and grab her hand. I give her a quick squeeze before asking, "You ready to go?" I catch the look she gives me before she's able to wipe it off and put on something more neutral. The adoration she was just showing only proves to me that this is something real.

"Yeah, let's go. I need a shower and to take off these heels," Grace says, squeezing my hand back.

I smile down at her and then look up to see my mom watching us. "Goodnight, mother. We'll see you tomorrow."

"Bye, you two. Get some rest. See you first thing, Grace!" We both smile back at her, waving our goodbye. We ease toward the exit, giving quick hugs and farewells. It's nice that we're not having to force time together from every moment this weekend. My family is content with quality time, rather than the quantity of it.

By the time we've made our way to the car, we're both quiet. Thankfully, Grace hasn't dropped my hand though. I hold her tight until I open her door and usher her into her seat. She opens her mouth to say something, but decides against it, turning to the front and buckling herself in.

I make my way around the car, forcing deep breaths into my too-tight lungs. I am *this close* to losing it. But we can't have the conversation that we need to have if either of us loses our heads.

The five minute trip back to the hotel is filled with silence, but not as tense as it could be, thankfully. I can tell that she has just as much on her mind, if not more. She's fidgeting, pulling her bracelet around her wrist over and over.

We're nearly back to the hotel when I see a small shape on the side of the road. I know if she sees it, she'll be upset. A distraction seems necessary. She's just moved from twirling her ring to looking out the window. It's amazing how many fidget toys she literally keeps on her body, disguised as jewelry.

"So, I was supposed to ask you if you wanted to go to the spa tomorrow, but I guess my mom beat me to it, huh?" I say, trying to draw her attention away from the window and the side of the road.

She's still turned away when she responds, "Hmm? Oh yeah, we were just discussing plans for tomorrow and she mentioned you'd be gone in the morning." She finally turns to look at me, but my relief is short-lived when she says, "I guess you were just going to leave me in the hotel room to find my own thing to do?" I flinch slightly, because *ouch.*

"No, actually I had completely forgotten about golfing. In the rush to get packed, get here and then my excitement in having you all to myself again after Ansley left, I just forgot. I was only reminded tonight when Kiera mentioned it. And then asked about your plans and if you'd want to do the spa day with them. It seems like something that would be good for you, though. So I'm glad you'll be able to go. You need some girl time and some time to be pampered. I'm sorry I haven't made that a priority for you." I say, trying to be honest with her and myself. "I'm sorry about a lot of things as far as the way this relationship has gone the last week."

"You're regretting it all, just now?" Grace asks, fully facing me and crossing her arms across her chest.

"What?" I nearly shout. "No, that's not what I'm saying at all. I mean...ugh. Can we have this conversation back in the room? Look there's the parking garage and we can go upstairs and I can actually look at you while we're talking. Please."

"Sure. That's fine. I know we need to talk," she says.

The silence is stilted now, broken only by the closing of car doors and the shuffle of our feet towards the elevator bank.

"Thanks," Grace says, a little under her breath.

"For what?" I ask, genuinely confused.

"For keeping my mind off of whatever cute little fur ball was dead on the road back there. I only caught a glimpse of it, but I knew you had probably already seen and that's why you started a conversation. I'm also sorry. That I snapped at you. But we can talk fully upstairs okay? I need to change into something comfortable before we dive in."

"Oh. Um, anytime. And nothing to apologize for. It's been a long day, a long week really. A lot of emotions already and some unsorted shit that needs to be sifted through," I say, trying to acknowledge feelings while still trying to underline our need to talk this out.

As I slip the key card back into my wallet, I open the door and let Grace walk through. I use the unguarded moment to once again admire the way she looks in this dress. But to be completely honest, I'm ready to see her in her ratty pajama pants and loose t-shirt that she sleeps in. She's even more beautiful when she's not trying.

Grace slips into the bathroom, quietly closing the door behind her. I can't remember the last time we used doors to separate ourselves, but if she feels that she needs that space, I won't be the one to impose. Instead, I walk over to the closet, sliding open the door and pulling out the hangers for my clothes that I wore tonight.

My dress pants are halfway down my legs when Grace comes out of the bathroom in nothing but a lacy black negligee. My movements are halted, my eyes the only thing that can find the willpower to roam. I feel my breath quicken and my briefs grow increasingly tighter.

"What are you—you look—Grace." Words tumble from my mouth with no coherency.

"You okay over there? You look like you need some help," she says, sashaying my way, causing me to stumble back a step onto the bed.

My pants are down around my ankles, my hands braced back on the bed. Grace drops to her knees in front of me, smirking up at my shocked face. She begins to work the material off my legs, freeing me for movement.

My brain must have short-circuited, because all of the words that I usually know how to say are completely gone from my mind. Watching Grace move in front of me is mesmerizing. Her eyes track my tongue as it comes out to wet my lips. I open my mouth to attempt one of those words I used to know, like *what* or *why*, but Grace rises, using her palms on my thighs to pull up. She places her mouth over mine, slotting us together perfectly.

I've lost all sense of control at this point, my hands fly to Grace's hips, lifting her up to straddle me. A soft gasp escapes her lips, setting me on fire.

We're quickly a clash of tongues and teeth, hands pulling and pushing everywhere. In one swift movement, I pull Grace off of my lap and flip us. Her back hits the comforter and I gently lower myself on top of her. Her eyes are wide and hungry, our breaths are mingled and the heat pouring off of both of us is insane. So it's amazing, even to me, when I hold myself a few inches off of her and say, "We really do need to talk, Grace."

Grace huffs a breath, blowing her hair out of her face. She's spread out beneath me, her breasts pressed up by the negligee and heaving with her breath. It's instinct to drop down and press kisses to the skin spilling out of her top, up onto her neck and finally, to her lips.

"You know that I want you. That's not what we need to talk about, buddy."

"I know, I know. I just thought...I don't know. I just thought that I could distract you for a little bit longer. Hold this off until later," Grace says, her eyes dipping down to skirt my gaze.

I place a finger under her chin, bringing her eyes back to mine. "Talk first, then maybe play later? How does that sound?"

"Well, sure. If you still want to later. We don't know how this conversation is going to go," she hedges.

"Only one way to find out," I remind her. And with that, I pull her up into a sitting position and hand her a big t-shirt. I'm not going to be able to focus when she's wearing next to nothing. In return, she reaches over and throws some pajama pants at me. *Touché.*

Chapter 52

Grace

This is not how I wanted tonight to go. I wanted to come back to the hotel and show Weston that I could still provide him with the physical part of our relationship even if we weren't going to be *together*. Instead, he's foregoing that to talk and I'm not sure what to think. Is he ending everything? Like no talk, no touch kind of rules?

Regardless of what I told him earlier when I was angry or what I've been trying to tell myself, I'll take whatever I can get from this relationship at this point. I can't lose Wes and whatever our friendship looks like now.

"So," he starts, a slight blush in his cheeks from our recent activity. "I think we should talk about what's going on between us. I'm afraid that we're both feeling and expecting different things at this point and I think that it would be wise to address those things before they fester and we lose something special."

Sitting on the bed, facing Weston as he says this, I can see the earnest and sincere love written all over his face. "So, where do you feel like you're at? I'm not ready to lose you as a friend.

Not now, not ever," I say, trying to put all of my cards on the table.

Weston straightens up, reaching out for my hands as he says, "Grace, you are never going to lose me. Unfortunately for you, you're stuck with me. I love you, Grace. You're my best friend and I don't want to spend any more days on this Earth not by your side. You're never getting rid of me."

A startled sob erupts from my chest, pulling my lips into a frown with their escape.

Wes pulls me to him, wrapping me into a bear hug and burying my face into his chest. "Oh, buddy, don't cry. It's going to be okay. We're going to be okay." He runs his hands through my hair, letting me continue to cry against him.

"I'm not sad, I'm overwhelmingly happy. After being so upset yesterday, this is just a lot of emotional instability and it's causing me to cry. But Weston, I am so incredibly happy · to hear you say that. I have been in love with you for way longer than I'd care to admit right now. You're stuck with me, too. Lucky you," I say, sniffling and leaning back to run my hands under my eyes. I try to keep the snot at bay, but it comes pouring out with the tears. "You get *all this*," I finish with a gesture to my blubbering self.

"I am one lucky man, indeed." Weston uses his thumbs to swipe away the remaining tears before leaning toward me and kissing me senseless.

"Can I...um...go to the bathroom real quick?" I ask, giggling in a near hysterical way.

"Oh! Of course!" Wes says, shepherding me up and off the bed. I look down and realize I'm still wearing his t-shirt over my lingerie. My giggling reaches a new level and I double over in a fit of laughter.

Before I take another step, I'm scooped up into a pair of strong arms, my head resting on my favorite chest. "Shh," Wes says, "I got you. Let's get you in the bath."

I don't know how he knows what to do, I've never had one of the near-panic episodes with him before. But, that's definitely what's happening. I can already feel the gasping starting. Tears are streaming down my face again. It sounds like I'm still laughing, but I'm not.

I'm lowered to my feet, my t-shirt and lingerie stripped off and I'm placed into an already full bath tub. Time must be moving at a different speed than I am right now.

Chapter 53

Weston

I've never seen Grace have a panic attack. But they're very similar to the ones that Autumn used to have. I remember when I was younger, I would watch our dad pull her out of an attack using grounding techniques. I don't know what grounds Grace, but I thought warmth couldn't hurt. I've lowered her into the bathtub, her stare still a thousand yards away from me.

I try to move back from the tub to give her space, but she pulls me closer. Her hands are scrabbling for purchase on my forearms, so I slip into the tub behind her. I readjust us so that I can hold her in my lap. My pajama pants are soaked, but that's a problem for later. Right now, I just need Grace to breathe.

I try to remember all of the things I saw my dad and then Robert do for Autumn. Robert has been Autumn's rock and grounding touch for most of my life it feels like. I pull Grace into my chest and stretch one of her hands out to the water. I whisper softly in her ear, "You feel the water? You feel my hand? You feel the edge of the tub? Can you smell the soap? Hear the drip of the water?" I'm trying to focus on any sensory input I can, knowing this is a technique I've seen and read about many times.

It takes Grace a minute, but eventually she's nodding, touching the water and my hand. Then reaching out to run her hand along the cold edge of the tub. It's another minute before she turns to me, her gaze back on mine and I breathe out a sigh of relief.

"What happened?" Grace asks, her voice soft.

"You had a panic attack. Have you ever had one before?" I ask, rearranging us to bring her face more in line with mine.

She shakes her head, though I can see she's thinking about past events that probably mirrored this. "Well, maybe once or twice in college. But I was alone—I only remember feeling overcome with thoughts and emotions and then I would wake up on the bathroom floor. I thought it was just like stress or something..."

"Well it can definitely be triggered by stress, and having unrelieved stress makes you more susceptible because you're unable to control your emotional response like you'd be able to normally," I say, smoothing her wet hair back from her forehead before placing a soft kiss there. "How are you feeling now?"

"Better, definitely better. How did you know what to do so quickly?" Grace asks, her face crinkling in confusion. She glances down and notices that I'm still in my pants. "And you're all wet! Oh no, let's get out," she says, starting to rise from my lap.

"No ma'am. Just a little longer until your pulse slows. I can still see it thumping in your neck." She settles back into my chest and I continue talking, trying to sooth her. "My oldest sister, Autumn, used to have panic attacks all the time when she was in high school. My dad was the one who could ground her. And then Robert came along and was her rock from then on. We've always been so grateful for Robert, especially after we lost my dad and Autumn kept suffering attacks. She's in therapy now and has a lot of calming and grounding techniques. We should talk to her sometime to see what she's learned that might help you."

Grace looks at me with so much love in her eyes, it makes it hard not to just kiss her right now—and I tell her just that. "I really want to kiss you, but I don't know if you're up to that yet."

"Oh. Um, yeah I think I'm definitely okay with a kiss," she replies after assessing her breathing and pulse for herself. "But, I do want to get out of this tub at some point, too. Especially since you're still wearing those flannel pants."

"Of course, my love," I say, pressing a kiss to her sweet mouth while rising from the water with her in my arms. I'm not ready to let go of her yet. Or ever.

"Buddy?" Grace says, a small smirk curving her lips.

"Yes?"

"I love you." Her eyes light up as she says it. "I've been waiting forever to tell you. And now that I can, I don't think I'm going to stop."

"I'm okay with that. I love you, too. A whole hell of a lot." A smile pulls all the way across my face. Grace wiggles and I reluctantly set her on her feet.

"Let's get you out of these soggy bottoms, shall we?" Grace gives me an evil grin as she drops to her knees on the bath mat to strip me out of my pants.

We both struggle to catch our breath, tangled in sheets and in need of another shower. Without even talking about it, I know this is more how Grace saw tonight ending. The permanent grin she has etched into her face says it all.

"So," I start, unsure how to even begin this conversation. "I know we started talking about the future sometime last month and that sort of stalled out. Now that I know you actually *like me*, can we talk about next steps?"

"Of course! I would love to. And to be clear, you've always known that I *liked* you."

"Well, *to be clear*, I much prefer the other 'L-word' coming out of your mouth," I say with a wink.

"I love you, weirdo," Grace replies, nuzzling into my neck and yawning like crazy.

"I know. But you know what? Let's save the future talks for tomorrow though? You've gotta be exhausted and I'm tired now that you're snuggled up against me. Sleep now, talk later?" I pull her tighter against me and let out a sigh of relief as she relaxes fully into me.

Chapter 54

Grace

It's amazing how much better I sleep when I'm enveloped in Weston's warmth. His touch, and the fact that even if we didn't resolve every issue, we are at least on the same page. I don't know exactly where our future is heading at this point, but I know it'll be somewhere together.

Weston stretches out underneath me, looking every bit a sleeping Greek god. The sun is shining directly across him from the window, bathing him in golden light. His light brown hair is hanging across his forehead, tousled from sleep. I reach over and push a lock of it away from his face, laying a tender kiss to his cheek.

"Mmm, you're awake?" Weston asks in his husky morning voice.

"I am, are you?" I ask with a laugh.

"Awake enough. I didn't hear either of our alarms, what time is it?" He rolls over to face me, running his fingers up and down my spine. I shiver in response, pulling a little growl from Weston's throat.

I giggle again, feeling lighter than air. I float back to Earth, saying, "I believe it is just before seven. What time do you need to be ready for golf? Did you even bring golfing clothes?"

"Well, I have khaki shorts, a polo and tennis shoes. That'll just have to do," he responds with a shrug and a small smile. A mischievous little grin takes over before he asks, "Did you bring spa clothes?"

"You mean my naked body? Yes, I got that with me, for sure." I watch as the heat enters Weston's eyes before I shake my head and laugh. "No sir. We are not getting started this morning. We have places to be and I'm about to be spending hours with your mom and sisters. I need time to collect myself!"

I throw the covers back, rushing out from underneath them before Weston can make a grab for me. He laughs loudly and I look behind me to see him fall back to the bed in a plush mound of pillows. I make my way to the bathroom, intending to take a nice, quiet shower to help clear my head. Before I can even turn the water on, however, a pair of strong hands grabs my waist, pulling me back into a hard body.

"Can I at least admire your spa get-up while you get all sudsy?" Weston asks, his voice low in my ear. A shiver runs down my spine and continues into my lower belly when his hands begin to roam.

"If—and only if—you can keep your hands to yourself," I say, admonishing him slightly as I step away. Maybe putting distance between us will calm my fraying nerves.

"Yes ma'am. I'll be on my best behavior," Weston says with a definite darkness to his voice.

"Mhm. I'll believe it when I see it," I snark, pulling my hair up into a messy bun to make sure it doesn't get wet.

I step under the spray, letting it wash over my chest and

feeling the immediate release of any built up tension in my body.

"God, why do you feel the need to shower in the eternal pits of Hell?" Weston nearly shouts as he climbs in with me. I just laugh, knowing he'll eventually adjust to the temperature.

Within seconds of him joining me, Weston is dropping kisses to my exposed neck and shoulders. "Hey, hey, hey, what are you doing? You're not even *trying* to behave," I berate him, barely suppressing a shiver.

"You only asked for my hands to stay away from you, you said nothing about my mouth." Weston's face is taken over by the sexiest smirk I have ever seen. And before I can say anything else, he backs me against the wall of the shower and sinks to his knees in front of me. "You gonna tell me to behave now?"

"Oh shut up and put that mouth to better use," I say, threading my hands into his hair and savoring the feeling of his lips on me.

➤➤

After our longer-than-necessary shower, it's time to start getting ready to head down to the spa. I'm still a little nervous, knowing that his family is probably going to have a lot of questions for me. But, I manage to tamp down the anxiety by grounding myself with our conversation last night.

"You ready?" Weston asks, running his hand through his light brown locks and grinning at me. *Handsome devil*, I think and smile back at him. "It's time for me to meet the guys downstairs for golf and I thought I'd drop you off at the spa so you didn't have to walk by yourself. Unless you need some alone time first, of course," he adds.

"Aww, that's sweet. I would love for you to walk me there.

Thanks, buddy," I answer, once again reveling in how sweet this man can be. That thought is immediately replaced with giggles as Weston smacks my legging-clad butt and heads to the door.

The spa is on the second floor and when the elevator stops to let us off, I'm suddenly nervous again. Weston must notice because he takes my hand and leads me toward the double doors at the end of the hallway.

"You're gonna be okay, buddy. You know they love you, just be yourself," he says, dropping a kiss on top of my head.

"Well yeah. But, they think we've been actually dating this whole time and I just know they're all going to be ravenous for information. I won't know what to tell them when they start asking for our future plans," I reply, fidgeting with my rings on my right hand.

"You tell them we're taking it slow and figuring it out as we go. That's not a lie, because that's exactly what's going to happen. There's no reason to worry. And worst case scenario? They don't get all their answers and they'll live. It's going to be okay. Now march your cute little ass in there and get to relaxing. You deserve it."

I blush and nod, knowing there's really nothing else to say. Why am I so worried about this, anyway?

"And hey, I love you," Weston says, causing me to blush even harder. I don't know if I'm going to get used to him saying that to me anytime soon.

"I love you, too. I can't wait to hear how badly you lose today," I say, a grin splitting my face.

"Oh, don't worry. I'm going to kill it," he says, turning me and patting my butt a little lighter than he did in the room. "You know I don't lose."

And with that, I walk into the spa to face the family of the man I've been dating for all of 12 hours.

Chapter 55

Grace

"Well look at who the cat dragged in," Kiera says, pulling me into a fierce hug. "I'm so glad that you could make it!"

"Me too!" I reply enthusiastically. And upon reflection, I notice that I am glad. Some of my anxiety ebbed just from talking to Weston about it.

"Grab a drink and head this way. We'll get you into a cute little robe and get ourselves some pampering."

"You don't have to tell me twice," I laugh. I inspect the little drink table they have set up on the side, landing on a cranberry mimosa. I bring the glass to my mouth, letting the bubbles from the champagne erupt over my tongue and release a silent sigh.

"Come on girls!" Rebecca shouts from the adjoining room.

Kiera gives me a wince and then a smile before saying, "Sorry, I know we said 8, but mom got here half an hour ago. She's on her third mimosa and ready for a pedicure."

"Hey, I'm ready for that, too," I say with a shrug and a smile. I am not one to judge. "And maybe a morning buzz isn't the worst idea."

"Hate to say this since it's my little brother and all, but, it kinda looks like you got a morning buzz already started," she replies, winking at me with a wolfish smile on her face.

I can't help the guffaw of laughter that comes from my belly and ricochets around the small room. Kiera just continues smiling, reveling in being so obviously right.

"What's so funny over there? You're welcome to share with the class," Tessa says from her spot in the corner of the couch. Her face is clouded with suspicion and it immediately sobers me. What does she know, or think she knows? I make a mental note to ask Weston later if this particular sister has something against me.

I shake off these thoughts, trying to settle into my role of the little brother's girlfriend and remember that I knew what I was getting myself into this morning.

Rebecca calls me over to where she's standing, holding her arms out for a hug. "Oh, Gracie, we're so glad you're here. For so many reasons. But I think we can all agree that we've never seen Weston happier than we have this weekend. So thank you for that."

I blush furiously, but make the mistake of looking away and towards Tessa. Who happens to be scowling in my direction. She doesn't even try to hide it when I look her way. I'm not the only one who notices, either.

"Hey, what's that face?" Autumn asks Tessa, giving her a questioning glance before following her line of sight to my face. Confusion mars Autumn's beautiful features before Carmen steps over and gets in Tessa's face. I can't hear what they're saying but it seems heated from here.

"Okay, there's something I think we need to talk about. And

now that we're all here, it seems like a good time," Tessa says as she rises from the couch. She downs the last few sips of her mimosa before setting the glass on the table and clasping her hands in front of her. "Grace, why are you lying to us?"

The silence in the room grows oppressive and it feels as if it could strangle me. I barely choke out the words, "I'm sorry, what?"

Carmen shakes her head at Tessa, but she is undeterred. "Why are you lying to us, telling us that you and Weston are dating? This is odd and a very mean thing to do to a family on a weekend that is supposed to be happy for them."

I am shocked to my core, unable to do anything but shake my head.

Kiera comes up behind me, putting a hand on my shoulder and turning me to face her. "Grace, what's she talking about? You and Wes aren't together? Why would you two tell us you're dating if you're not?" Genuine hurt flashes across Kiera's face before she reins it back in. "You can talk to us, but please be honest."

I take a deep breath, looking around the room filled with the most important people in Weston's life. I settle my gaze on Tessa before I finally answer, "It's not a lie. We are together."

Tessa huffs and turns to their mother. "Mom, Weston told me last night that they were faking a relationship because we put too much pressure on him to have someone. But what I can't figure out is, why *she* would go along with it," she finishes, gesturing at me. Holding my gaze she asks, "Did you do all of this for a free weekend in So-Cal? If so, that's just pathetic. Why would you string my brother along like this? After he admitted the ruse last night, he also told me that he's fallen for you. You're going to hurt him."

She's not saying anything that hadn't already crossed my mind, but she also has outdated information.

Rebecca has lost all of the color in her face and is staring at me with her mouth agape. "Grace?"

"Okay, let's just get this over with. This did start as a fake relationship. Weston didn't want to show up without a date and it was convenient because we were already traveling together for work. We went into this as friends, but we're so much more now. Tessa, I need to thank you. I think whatever you said to him last night got through, because we finally talked. As of last night, we *are* together. I love him. I love your brother and your son. I love him so much it hurts. We may have started this with no intention of ending up here, but here we are regardless. And if you all are not okay with that, I suggest you get okay with it. I'm not going to be letting him go now that I have him. He's my best friend, the love of my life and I'm not losing him."

The silence that fills the room this time is so electrically charged, I'm afraid I might get shocked. One moment, I'm staring into five sets of disbelieving eyes, so like Weston's. And the next, I'm being ambushed by bodies. There are arms thrown around my neck, my shoulders, my waist. My face is wet with tears and I hear the unmistakable sound of sniffles surrounding me.

"Oh no, Grace. I am so, so sorry. I am such an ass. I thought you were just leading him on. He's my little brother. But you really do love him," Tessa says, gripping the back of my head as she pulls me even tighter into a hug.

"I really do," I sob. "I thought I was going crazy, falling in love with a fake boyfriend. But it was never really untrue. The feelings have been there the whole time." I look at Rebecca, wiping her eyes with one hand while rubbing my back with the other. "You raised such an incredible man. You all did," I say, meeting all of his sisters' eyes.

We continue to embrace each other for a few more minutes, settling into it. Someone on the couch clears their throat and we all turn to look at Lisa who has made her way back to the seating area. "Well, that was an unexpected start to the day. Drinks, anyone?" she asks, raising a full glass of champagne to the group.

"Hell yes," Carmen replies, walking back to her wife. Glasses are passed around and we're sitting in a circle, facing each other and smiling.

"To love?" Tessa offers.

"To love," we reply in chorus before laughing and tipping our drinks back.

Chapter 56

Weston

I hear the electric sounds of the door unlocking before several giggling voices float into the room. I expected Grace back about an hour ago, but I assumed she'd been caught up with the girls—and it looks like I was right. Following her into our room are all of my sisters, my sister-in-law and my mother, all laughing and yet to notice that I'm sitting here staring at them.

Grace's eyes meet mine and her beautiful smile only grows brighter. "There he is, ladies. Let him have it," she says, crossing her arms over her chest, but not dropping her grin.

I'm thoroughly confused and I know it's showing on my face. Tessa pounces on me from across the room, tickling the hell out of my stomach. I'm sucking in air and begging for reprieve by the time she moves off of me, saying, "You're such a brat!"

"You're going to have to be more specific. Why are you all in here and staging what feels like an intervention?" I ask, still extremely confused and now holding my stomach like I can get more air into my lungs with the pressure.

"You made us attack Grace this morning!" Tessa yells at me

before turning a sympathetic look to the woman in question.

"To be fair, Tess, you were the only one on the attack," Autumn murmurs. Tessa shoots her a withering glare and Autumn just shrugs.

Kiera comes closer, sitting gently on the edge of the bed. "I'm sorry you felt that you had to lie to us to make us happy. And I'm sorry that you got caught up in this, Grace," she says softly.

"Son, why would you lie to us about this? Have we really made it that hard to be honest with us about your love life? I understand that we pester you more than necessary, we just want you to be happy. But that doesn't mean that we want to force you into something you don't want." At this, she glances between me and Grace before continuing, "No one is going to say anything if you need to stage a little break-up so you don't have to continue this farce."

I sit up in bed so fast I dislodge Kiera from her perch. I'm on my feet, walking towards Grace before I can even fully comprehend the words coming from my mother's mouth. My hands shoot out, grabbing hers, pulling her to me and to the shelter of my body. I study her face, seeing only love there.

I turn to face my family. My very nosy, very loving family. "I love Grace. I know we started this with a lie, but I've never felt anything more true in my life. She's mine and I'm hers and this is real. I'm sorry for lying to you all, and I'm sorry that Grace had to contribute to that lie. But, I wouldn't take back a single minute of it." I hug Grace even further into my side, not letting her even attempt to gain space.

"Well good, now we've got that settled," Mom says, chuckling. My sisters all have tears in their eyes and are smiling like crazy.

"Did you just trick me into admitting my feelings in front of the group? That feels unfair," I muse.

"Almost as unfair as thinking you two were together this entire time and knowing that you should be. You're perfect together and we're just happy that you've finally seemed to figure that out," Carmen says, arching a brow at me.

"Touché, big sis," I laugh out.

My eyes roam the gathered group—all of my most important people in one room—and I can't help the stupid grin that overtakes my face. I look at Kiera and say, "So does this mean I'm excused from giving a speech tonight?" They all burst into laughter and close in on me and Grace, smothering us with their love.

"Absolutely not, little brother," Kiera answers, huffing out a sigh when she's pushed into the middle of our group hug.

Chapter 57

Weston

I wake up on Sunday morning and watch as the sun rises over the edge of the window, laying its rays gently on Grace's skin. The beauty of this moment is indescribable and though I've never been creative like the woman laying next to me, I wish I could somehow preserve this. Maybe I'll get into photography—or I'll just have to make sure we continue to have moments like these to savor.

Grace begins to stir next to me, no doubt awoken by my intent staring. She always seems to be able to feel when I'm awake and looking at her.

"Morning, buddy," she says, sleepily.

"Good morning, beautiful. How did you sleep?" I ask, slowly moving over her. I begin kissing from one shoulder, across her chest to the other. I nip at her collarbone, pulling a sweet moan from her lips.

"Um, I slept well. I'm liking being awake better, though," Grace answers, breath catching.

➥

"So, Miss Herrera, now that you've met the entire extended family and conquered their hearts, what are your plans?" I ask once we're laying under the sheets again. Grace is in my arms and I'm tracing lazy patterns on her back.

"Mmm, Disney World? Isn't that what I'm supposed to say?"

I burst into laughter, not expecting the football reference, but loving her more for it. "I was thinking more, where do you want to go for our next assignment? I've seen several in the Northeast and several in the South if you're looking for something warm," I reply.

"I want to go home," she says softly. My fingers stop their idle movements, waiting for her to continue. "I want you to take me home. Let's find somewhere to settle, at least for now. I want something permanent with you."

I intake a sharp breath, trying not to overwhelm her with emotion. "Are you sure? You won't get too bored?"

"With you? Never. You're my best friend. I know wherever you are, is where I want to be. Just one request?" Grace turns her face to mine, looking a bit sheepish.

I'm reluctant to ask, fearing it might be something hard to grant. "Yes?"

"Can we get a kitten?" Her dark brown eyes are alight with hope and there's no way I'm ever going to be able to tell this woman no. Maybe it'll at least take her some time before she realizes she has me wrapped around her little finger.

"Of course we can. As long as you don't name him something nerdy," I tease.

"No promises on that one," she says through her giggles. She suddenly pops up, taking my hands with her. She's bouncing in the bed, making me laugh along with her.

"What's all this about?" I ask, trying to keep her from falling backwards in her excitement.

"I just can't wait to start the rest of our lives together. It makes me so happy," she replies simply.

"Me too, buddy," I say, pulling her back down and rolling her to her back before showing her just how happy she makes me.

Epilogue

Grace

"Ahh! I cannot wait!" I screech at the phone.

Lexa's laugh filters through the line and I can hear Drew asking if she's talking to a pterodactyl. I can't help it though. Drew and Lexa are getting married and I get to be a part of their day.

Drew's voice gets closer to the phone and he says, "Is Weston nearby?"

"Of course! Let me grab him," I reply, putting my hand over the microphone on the cell so I can yell for Wes.

He comes trotting in from the living room, a look of slight alarm on his face. "What's up? I heard screaming."

"Here, just take this," I say, handing him the phone.

"Hey, it's Weston," he says, still looking me over for any indication of injury.

His expression morphs from concern into pure joy and I know that Drew just asked him to be a groomsman. "Dude, I would be honored. Congratulations, you two! We can't wait."

They talk for another minute before Weston hands the phone

back to me. Lexa and I chat a bit, catching up on other recent life events and I squeal one more time for good measure. Wes and Lexa just laugh, indulging my happiness.

When we hang up, Weston grabs me up into a hug and squeezes me to him. "Our friends are getting married!" he says with a huge smile on his face. And this is just one more thing I love about him. His genuine love and happiness for his friends is a sight to behold.

"Meow?" Our heads turn in the direction of the little sound. Weston sets me down to pick up the newest member of our household. "Hey little Frodo," he says, scratching our little brown kitten behind the ears. So much for not having a nerdy name, but it fits him so well with his sweet brown curls. His hair is only one shade darker than Weston's and it's the cutest thing to see them together.

"Oh, hold right there!" I say, grabbing my phone to snap a quick picture. I examine the lighting and give Weston a quick thumbs up. I can't wait to paint that scene while in my little studio in the backyard. Weston built it for me the first week we were here.

I've never been happier to be settled somewhere. A beautiful studio, a sweet little kitten and my best friend. Forever.

About the Author

Leah Beach is a contemporary romance author, writing about your every day love stories. Originally from North Alabama, she moved south to the beach after finishing nursing school and marrying the love of her life. She and her husband currently coach high school girl's soccer in between Leah's shifts in the ER.

Leah is a self-published author who began writing as a way to help her mental health. She has continued to write, loving to have her words out in the world.

Be on the lookout for more of Leah's works, coming soon! (Including a fun thriller in the works!)

Also by Leah Beach

To Those Who Wait

After 10 years of being unlucky in love, Lexa Chase and Drew Parker are finally ready to give their relationship a chance.

Will their luck turn around or will their long-term friendship crash and burn?

Available on Amazon.com and BarnesandNoble.com

www.ingramcontent.com/pod-product-compliance
Lightning Source LLC
Chambersburg PA
CBHW032235310726
48973CB00008B/2144